# THE UNDER DOG

Also by Markus Zusak:

*Fighting Ruben Wolfe*
*Getting the Girl*

*The Book Thief*

# THE UNDER DOG

MARKUS ZUSAK

Definitions

THE UNDERDOG
A DEFINITIONS BOOK 978 1 849 41699 3

Originally published in Australia in 1999 by Pan Books,
an imprint of Pan Macmillan Australia.

Published in Great Britain in 2013 by Definitions,
an imprint of Random House Children's Publishers UK
A Random House Group Company

1 3 5 7 9 10 8 6 4 2

The Random House Group Limited supports the Forest Stewardship Council (FSC®), the
leading international forest certification organization. Our books carrying the FSC label are
printed on FSC®-certified paper. FSC is the only forest certification scheme endorsed by the
leading environmental organizations, including Greenpeace. Our paper procurement policy can
be found at www.randomhouse.co.uk/environment.

MIX
Paper from
responsible sources
FSC® C016897

Set in Perpetua

Definitions are published by Random House Children's Publishers UK,
61–63 Uxbridge Road, London W5 5SA

www.randomhousechildrens.co.uk
www.totallyrandombooks.co.uk
www.randomhouse.co.uk

Addresses for companies within The Random House Group Limited can be found at:
www.randomhouse.co.uk/offices.htm

THE RANDOM HOUSE GROUP Limited Reg. No. 954009

A CIP catalogue record for this book is available from the British Library.

Printed and bound by CPI Group (UK) Ltd, Croydon, CR0 4YY

*For my family*

# 1

We were watching the telly when we decided to rob the dentist.

'The dentist?' I asked my brother.

'Sure, why not?' was his reply. 'Do you know how much money goes through a dental surgery in a day? It's obscene. If the prime minister was a dentist, the country wouldn't be in the state it's in right now, I can tell you. There'd be no unemployment, no racism, no sexism. Just money.'

'Yeah.'

I agreed with my brother Ruben only to keep him happy. The truth was that he was just grandstanding again. It was one of his worst habits.

That was the first truth, of two.

The second was that even though we had decided to knock over our local dentist, we were never going to do it. So far this year we'd promised to rob the bakery, the fruit shop, the hardware, the fish 'n' chip shop, and the optometrist. It never happened.

'And this time I'm serious.' Rube sat forward on the couch. He must have been seeing what I was thinking.

We weren't robbing anything.

We were hopeless.

Hopeless, pitiful, and a shake-your-head kind of pathetic.

I myself had a job twice a week delivering newspapers but I got sacked after I broke some guy's kitchen window. It wasn't even a hard throw. It just happened. The window was there half open, I threw the paper, and *smack!* It went through the glass. The bloke came running out and went berserk and hurled abuse at me as I stood there with a pile of ridiculous tears in my eyes. The job was gone – cursed from the start.

My name's Cameron Wolfe.

I live in the city.

I go to school.

I'm not popular with the girls.

I have a little bit of sense.

I don't have much sense.

I have thick, furry hair that isn't long but always looks messy and always sticks up, no matter how hard I try keeping it down.

My older brother Ruben gets me into plenty of trouble.

I get Rube into as much trouble as he gets me into.

I have another brother named Steve who's the oldest and is the winner of the family. He's had quite a few girls and has a good job and he's the one a lot of people like. He's also some kind of good footballer on top of it.

I have a sister named Sarah who sits on the couch with her boyfriend and has him stick his tongue down her throat whenever possible. Sarah's second oldest.

I have a father who constantly tells Rube and me to wash ourselves because he reckons we look filthy and stink like jungle animals crawling out of the mud.

('I don't bloody stink!' I argue with him. 'And I have a shower quite bloody regularly!'

'Well have you heard of soap? . . . I was once your age myself y' know, and I know how filthy guys your age are.'

'Is that right?'

'Of course it is. I wouldn't say it otherwise.'

No point arguing on.)

I have a mother who says very little but is the toughest thing in our house.

3

I have a family, yes, that doesn't really function without tomato sauce.

I like winter.

That's me.

Oh, and yeah, at the point in time I'm talking about, I had never, not even once, robbed a single thing in my life. I just talked about it with Rube, exactly like that day in the lounge room.

'Oi.'

Rube slapped Sarah on the arm as she kissed that boyfriend on our couch.

'Oi – we're gonna rob the dentist.'

Sarah stopped.

'Hey?' she enquired.

'Ah, forget it.' Rube looked away. 'Is this a useless house or isn't it? There are ignorant people everywhere, too busy with 'emselves to care.'

'Ah, stop whingein',' I told him.

He looked at me. That was all he did, as Sarah got back down to business.

I switched off the TV then and we left. We left to check out the dentist's surgery we were going to 'hit', as Rube put it. (The real reason we went there was just to get out of the house, because Sarah and her boyfriend were going insane in the lounge room and our mother was cooking mushrooms in the kitchen, which stank out the whole place.)

'Bloody mushrooms again,' I said as we walked out onto the street.

'Yeah,' Rube smirked. 'Just drown 'em in tomato sauce again so you can't taste 'em.'

'Bloody oath.'

What whingers.

'And there she is.' Rube smiled as we walked onto Main Street in the darkening air of June and winter. 'Doctor Thomas G. Edmunds. Bachelor of Dental Surgery. Beautiful.'

We started making a plan.

Plan-making between my brother and me consisted of me asking questions and Rube answering them. It went like this:

'Won't we need a gun or somethin'? Or a knife? That fake gun we had got lost.'

'It isn't lost. It's behind the couch.'

'Y' sure?'

'Yes. I'm sure . . . and in any case, we don't need it. All we need is the cricket bat and we'll get next-door's baseball bat, right?' He laughed, very sarcastically. 'We swing those babies a few times and they can't possibly say no.'

'OK.'

OK.

Yeah, right.

We scheduled everything for the next afternoon. We got the bats, we went over everything we had to remember, and we knew we weren't going to do it. Even Rube knew.

We went to the dentist next day anyway, and for the first time ever in one of our heists, we actually went inside.

What greeted us was a shock, because behind the counter was the most brilliant dental nurse you've ever seen. I'm serious. She was writing something with her pen and I couldn't take my eyes off her. Never mind about the baseball bat I was holding. I forgot all about it. There was no robbery. We just stood there, Rube and I.

Rube and I, and the dental nurse, in the room, together.

'Be with y' in a sec,' she said politely, without looking up. God almighty she was beautiful. Absolutely. Brilliant.

'Oi,' Rube whispered to her, really quiet. He was making sure only I could hear him. 'Oi . . . This is a holdup.'

She didn't hear.

'Stupid bloody cow.' He looked at me and shook his head. 'Y' can't even hold up a dentist any more. Sheez. What's the world comin' to?'

'Now.' She finally looked up. 'What can I do for you fellas?'

'Ah . . .' I was uneasy, but what else was I meant to say? Rube said nothing. There was silence. I had to break it. I smiled and fell apart. 'Ah, we just came to get a checkup.'

She smiled back. 'When would you like it?'

'Aah, tomorrow?'

'Four o'clock OK?'

'Yep.' I was nodding, wondering.

She looked into me. Right in. Waiting. Helpful. 'So what are your names?'

'Oh yeah,' I responded, laughing pretty stupidly. 'Cameron and Ruben Wolfe.'

She wrote it down, smiled again, and then spotted the cricket and baseball bats.

'Just been puttin' in some practice.' I lifted the baseball bat.

'In the middle of winter?'

'We can't afford a football,' Rube interrupted us. We had a football and a soccer ball somewhere in

our back yard. He pushed me towards the door.
'We'll be back tomorrow.'

She grinned her happy-I'm-here-to-help smile. She
said, 'OK, bye-ee.'

I stayed a second and said, 'Bye.'

Bye.

Could I think of nothing better?

'Y' bloody spastic,' Rube told me, once we were
back outside. 'Checkups,' he whined. 'The old man
wants us smellin' like roses, sure enough, but he's
not interested in us havin' clean teeth. He couldn't
give a bloody toss about our teeth!'

'Well, who got us in there to begin with, ay?
Whose great idea was it to rob the dentist? Not
bloody mine, mate!'

'OK, OK.' Rube leaned against the wall. Traffic
limped past us.

'And what the hell was all that whisperin'
about?'

I'd decided by now that while I had him against
the wall I'd go in for the kill. 'The only thing you
forgot to say was *please*. Maybe she'd have heard y'
then. *Oi, this is a holdup,*' I imitated him with a
whisper. 'Absolutely pathetic.'

Rube snapped. 'All right! I blew it . . . Still, I

didn't exactly see you swingin' that baseball bat.' This was better now for Rube, since we were back on what I did wrong as opposed to what he did. 'You didn't swing a thing, mate . . . You were too busy lookin' in Blondie's big blue eyes and starin' at her, her breasts.'

'I was *not!*'

Breasts.

Who was he kidding?

Talking like that.

'Oh yeah.' Rube kept laughing. 'I seen you, y' dirty little bastard.'

'Ah, that's lies.' But it wasn't. Walking down Main Street, I knew I was in love with the beautiful blonde dental nurse. I was already fantasizing about lying in the dentist chair with her over the top of me, on my lap, asking, 'Are y' comfortable, Cameron? Y' feeling nice?'

'Great,' I'd reply. 'Great.'

'Oi.'

'*Oi!*' Rube shoved me, 'Are you still listenin'?'

I turned back to him. He continued talking.

'So why don't y' tell me where the hell we're gonna get the money for these checkups, ay?' He thought about it for a minute as we started up walking again and quickened the pace for home. 'Nah, we're better off cancelling.'

'No,' I answered. 'No way Rube.'

'Dirty boy,' was his retort. 'Forget the nurse. She's prob'ly doin' it with Mister Doctor Dentist as we speak.'

'Don't you talk about her like that,' I warned him.

Rube stopped walking again.

Then he stared.

Then he said, 'You're pitiful, y' know that?'

'I know.' I could only agree. 'I guess you're right.'

'As always.'

We walked on. Again. Tail between the legs.

Oh, and by the way, we didn't cancel.

We considered asking our folks for the cash but they'd have wanted to know just why we went down there to begin with, and a discussion of that nature wasn't exactly high on our list. I myself got the money I needed by taking it out from my stash under the wrecked corner of carpet in our room.

We went back.

I tried like hell to keep my hair down. For the nurse.

We went back there the next day.

It didn't work – with the hair.

We went back there next day and there was a kind of beastly dental nurse there of about forty years of age.

'Now *there's* someone in your range,' Rube whispered at me in the waiting room. He was grinning like the dirty juvenile he had always been, He disgusted me, but then again, quite often, I disgusted myself.

'Hey,' I told him and waved a finger. 'I think you've got somethin' stuck in your teeth there.'

'Where?' He panicked. 'Here?' He opened his mouth and grimaced a wide smile. 'Is it gone?'

'Nah – further right. That way.' There was nothing there, of course, and when he looked at his reflection in the dental surgery fish tank and found out, he returned and slapped me across the back of the head.

'Huh.' He kept going with his original line. 'Y' dirty boy.' He chuckled. 'I'll admit it, though. She was good. She was fully great.'

'Mmm.'

'Not like middle-aged fat woman here, ay?'

I laughed. Boys like us – boys in general – would have to be the scum of the earth. Most of the time, any way. I swear it, we spend most of our time being inhumane.

We need a good kick in the pants, as my old man always says (and gives us).

He's right.

The nurse came in. 'Right, who's first?'

All quiet.

Then, 'Me.'

I stood up. I decided it would be best to get this over with quickly.

In the end, it wasn't too bad. There was just this fluoride treatment stuff that tasted pretty ordinary and some scratching around inside from the big man. There was no drill. Not for us. There is no justice in the world.

Or maybe there is . . .

The dentist ended up robbing *us*. He was pretty pricey, even for the little bit he did for us.

'All that money,' I said after we'd walked out again.

'Still' – Rube was finally the one not doing the complaining – 'no drill.' He punched my shoulder. 'I s'pose. No chocolate biscuits at our joint. It's good for somethin', ay. Good for the fangs . . . We've got a genius for a mother.'

I disagreed. 'Nah, she's just tight.'

We laughed, but we knew Mum was brilliant. It was just Dad that was a worry.

Back home, not much was going on. We could smell leftover mushrooms heating on the stove and Sarah was going at it on the couch again. No point going in.

I went into Rube's and my room and looked at the city that spread its filthy breath across the horizon. The sun was pale yellow behind it and the buildings were like the feet of huge black beasts lying down.

Yeah, it was around the middle of June at this time, and the weather was really starting to bite.

I guess things happened in my life that winter, but nothing too out of the ordinary. I failed in getting my old job back. My father gave me a chance. My elder brother Steve screwed up his ankle, insulted the hell out of me, and eventually came to realize something. My mother held a boxing exhibition in our school welfare office and went berserk one night, throwing the compost at my feet in the kitchen. My sister, Sarah, got jilted. Rube started growing a beard and eventually woke up to himself a bit. Greg, a guy who was once my best friend, asked me for three hundred bucks to save his life. I met a girl and fell in love with her (but then, I could fall in love with anything that showed an interest). I dreamed a whole lot of weird, sick, perverted, sometimes beautiful dreams. And I survived.

Nothing much happened really.

It was all pretty normal.

## FIRST DREAM:

*It's late afternoon and I'm walking to the dental surgery when I see someone standing on the roof. As I move closer I realize it's the dentist. I can tell from the white coat and the moustache. He's right on the edge, looking prepared to throw himself off.*

*I stop beneath him and yell, 'Oi! What the hell are you doing?'*

*'What's it look like?'*

*At that, I'm speechless.*

*All I can do now is run into the arcade building where the dental surgery is situated and go through and tell the beautiful dental nurse.*

*'What!' is her reply.*

*My God, she looks so great that I almost tell her, 'To hell with Mister Dentist, let's go down the beach or something.' I don't say anything else, though. I just run to the* end of a corridor, open the door, and take some stairs up to the roof.

For some reason, when I make it to the edge, the dental nurse hasn't come with me.

When I stand next to the brooding, moustached dentist and look over the edge, she's standing at the bottom, trying to tell him to come down.

'What are you doing down there?' I call down to her.

'I'm not going up there!' she shouts back up. 'I'm scared of heights!'

I accept her statement, because, quite frankly, I'm happy enough because I can see her legs and body, and my stomach tightens under my skin.

'Come on, Tom!' She tries to negotiate with the dentist, 'Come back down. Please!'

'Say, what are you doin' up here anyway?' I ask him.

He turns to face me.

Candid.

Then he says, 'It's because of you.'

'Me! What the hell did I do?'

'I overcharged you.'

'Geez, mate, that wasn't very nice,' and suddenly, sadistically, I urge him on. 'Go on, jump, then — you deserve it, you bloody cheat.'

*Even the beautiful dental nurse wants him to jump now. She calls out, 'Come on, Tom — I'll catch you!'*

*It happens.*

*Down.*

*Down.*

*He jumps and falls down, and the beautiful dental nurse catches him, kisses his mouth, and places him gently on the ground. She even holds him, touching bodies with him. Oh, that white uniform, rubbing on him. It drives me wild, and instantly, when she calls for me to jump as well, I do it and fall . . .*

*In bed, waking up, I'm lying there with the taste of blood in my mouth, and with the memory of footpath and impact in my head.*

# 2

Since the whole dentist incident drained my money situation, I pretty much went and begged for my old job back. The guy in the newsagent's wasn't impressed.

He said, 'Sorry, Mr Wolfe. You're just too much of a risk. You're dangerous.'

Have a listen to the bloke. You'd think I was walking around with a sawn-off shotgun or something. Bloody hell, I was just a paper boy.

'C'mon, Max,' I pleaded with him. 'I'm older now. More responsible.'

'How old are y' anyway?'

'Fifteen.'

'Well . . .' He thought hard. He stopped — drew the line. 'No.' He shook his head. 'No. No.' But I had him, surely. There was too much hesitation in him. He was thinking too hard. 'Fifteen's too old now, anyway.'

Too old!

Mate, it didn't feel too good to be a washed-up, redundant paper boy, I can tell you.

'Please?' I drooled. It was sickening. All this for a lousy paper run, while other guys my age were raking it in at Maccas and Kentucky Fried bloody Chickens. It was a disgrace. 'C'mon, Max.' I had an idea. 'If y' don't employ me again I'll come here wearin' these clothes I'm wearin' right now' (I was wearing crummy tracksuit pants, old shoes, and a dirty old spray jacket) 'and I'll bring my brother and his mates along and we'll treat the place like a library. We won't cause trouble, mind you. We'll just hang around. A few of 'em might steal, but I doubt it. Maybe just one or two . . .'

Max stepped closer.

'Are you threatenin' me, y' little grot?'

'Yes, sir, I am.' I smiled. I thought things were going along fine.

I was wrong.

I was wrong because my old boss Max took me by the collar of my jacket and removed me from his property.

'And don't come back in here again,' he ordered me.

I stood.

I shook my head.

At myself.

A grot. A grot!

It was true.

My game plan for getting the job back had back-fired miserably. The pulse in my neck felt really heavy, and I felt like I could taste last night's blood in the bottom of my throat.

'Y' grot,' I called myself. I looked at myself in the bakery shop window next door and imagined I was wearing a brand-new light blue suit with a black tie, black shoes, nice hair. The reality, though, was that I was wearing peasants' clothes and my hair was sticking up worse than ever. I looked at myself in that window, oblivious to all the people around me, and I stared and smiled that particular smile. You know that smile that seems to knock you and tell you how pathetic you are? That's the smile I was smiling.

'Yeah,' I said to myself. 'Yeah.'

I looked in the local paper – I had to get Rube to go in the newsagent's and buy it for me – for another job, but nothing was going. Things were skinny. Jobs. People. Values. No one was on the lookout for anyone or anything new. It got to the point where I considered doing the unthinkable – asking my father if I could work with him on Saturdays.

'No way,' he said, when I approached him. 'I'm a plumber, not a circus clown, or a zookeeper.' He was eating his dinner. He raised his knife. 'Now, if I was—'

'Ah, c'mon, Dad. I can help.'

Mum put in her opinion.

'Come on, Cliff, give the boy a chance.'

He sighed, almost moaned.

A decision: 'OK,' although he waved his fork under my nose. 'But all it'll take is one screwup, one smart-mouth remark, one act of stupidity, and you'll be out.'

'OK.'

I smiled.

I smiled to Mum but she was eating her dinner.

I smiled to Mum and Rube and Sarah and even to Steve, but they were all eating their dinner because the matter was over and the whole thing didn't really excite any of them. Only me.

Even at work on Saturday my father didn't seem too enthusiastic about me being there. The first thing he made me do was stick my hand down some old lady's toilet and pull all the blockage out. It's true, I nearly vomited into the bowl right there and then.

'Oh, blood-y *hell*!' I screeched under my breath, and my father just smiled.

He said, 'Welcome to the world, my boy,' and it was the last time he smiled at me all day. The rest of the time he made me do all the sap jobs like getting pipes off the roof of his panel van, digging a trench under a house, turning the mains off and on, and collecting and tidying his tools. At the end of the day he gave me twenty bucks and actually said thanks.

He said, 'Thanks for your help, boy.'

It shocked me.

Happy.

'Even though you *are* a bit slow.' He cut me down right after. 'And make sure you have a shower when we get home . . .'

During lunch it was funny because we sat on these two buckets at Dad's van and he made me read the paper. He took the Weekend Extra part out of the inside and threw the rest of it over to me.

'Read,' he told me.

'Why?'

'Because you don't learn anything unless you

can find the patience to read. TV takes that away from you. It robs you from your mind.'

No need to say that I stuck my head in that paper and read it. I could easily have been sacked for not reading the paper when I was told to.

The most important thing was that I survived the day and I had another twenty dollars to my name. 'Next Saturday?' I asked Dad when we got back out at home.

He nodded.

The thing is, I had no idea that this working Saturdays was going to lead me to the feet of a girl who was even better than the dental nurse. It was a few weeks away yet, but when it came I felt something shift inside me.

On that first Saturday night, though, I walked in our front door feeling quite proud of myself. I went down to the basement because it's Steve's room and Steve always goes out on Saturday nights, and I turned up his old stereo and moved around to it a bit. I sang along like all poor saps do in their own company, and I danced like a complete klutz. You don't care when there's no one around to look.

Then Rube came in, without me knowing.

He looked.

'Pitiful.' His voice shocked me.

I stopped.

'Pitiful,' he repeated, shutting the door and taking slow, deliberate paces down the old, worn steps.

He was followed in by Dad saying, 'I've got four things to say to you blokes. One, dinner's ready: Two, have showers. Three' — and he looked directly at Rube for this one — 'you — shave.' I looked briefly at Rube and saw patches of beard growing on his face. It was just becoming kind of thick and consistent. 'And four, we're watchin' *The Good, the Bad and the Ugly* tonight and if either one of you wants to watch something else, tough luck — the TV's booked.'

'We don't care,' Rube assured him.

'Just so there's no complaints.'

'Just so there *are* no complaints,' I corrected the man. Big mistake.

'Are you tryin' to start something?' He pointed as he came farther in.

'Not at all.'

He backed away. 'Well, good. Anyway, come to

dinner,' and as we walked towards him, he mentioned, 'Don't forget your old man can still give you a good kick in the pants for bein' smart.' He was laughing, though. I was glad.

At the door, I said, 'Maybe I'll save to get a stereo, like Steve's. A better one, maybe.'

Dad nodded. 'Not a bad idea." No matter how harsh the man could be, I guess he liked it that I never just asked for things. He saw that I wanted to earn them.

I did.

I wanted nothing for free.

Nothing came for free at our place anyway.

Rube spoke.

He asked, 'Why would you want a stereo for, boy? So you can dance up in our room as pitifully as *that*?'

Dad only stopped, looked back at him, and clipped him on the ear.

He said, 'At least the boy wants to work, which is more than I can say for you.' He turned away again and said, 'Now come for the dinner.'

We followed our father back up and I had to get

Sarah out of her room for dinner. She was in there with the boyfriend getting it off with him against the wardrobe.

*It's a movie scene in which I have a noose around my neck, waiting to be hanged. I'm sitting on a horse. The rope is attached to a heavy tree branch. My father is on a horse in the distance, waiting with a gun.*

*I know that there has been a price on my head for quite some time, and my father and I have a plan going where he turns me in, collects the reward, then shoots the rope as I'm about to be hanged. Somehow I will then get away and we will continue the process in towns all over the countryside.*

*I'm sitting there with that rope around my neck in a whole lot of outrageous cowboy gear. The sheriff or lawman or whoever he is is reading me the death sentence and all these tobacco-chewing country folk are cheering because they know I'm about to die.*

*'Any last words?' they ask me, but at first, I only laugh.*

*Then I say, still laughing, 'Good luck,' and with sarcasm, 'God bless.'*

*The shot should come any moment now. It doesn't.*

*I get nervous. I twitch.*

*I look around, and see him.*

*The horse is slapped, to make it take off, and next thing, I'm hanging there, choking to death.*

*My hands are tied in front of me and I reach them up to keep the rope off my neck. It isn't working. I gasp, horribly, saying, 'Come on! Come on.'*

*Finally.*

*The shot comes. Nothing.*

*'I'm still choking!' I hiss, but now my father is riding towards the mob. He fires again, and this time the rope is broken and I fall.*

*I hit the ground.*

*I suck.*

*Air.*

*Lovely.*

*Bullets fly all around me.*

*I reach for my father's hand and he lifts me onto his horse on the run.*

*Wide shot (camera shot).*

*New scene.*

*All is now calm and Dad holds about a dozen hundred-dollar notes in his hand. He gives me one.*

*'One!'*

*'That's right.'*

'You know,' I reason, 'I really think I should get more than just this — after all, it's my neck hangin' up there.'

Dad smiles and throws away a cigar, chewed.

He speaks.

'Yeah, but it's me who shoots you down.'

With desert all around me, I realize how sore my back is from falling down.

Dad is gone, and alone, I kiss the note and say, 'Damn you, my friend.' I begin walking somewhere, waiting for next time, hoping that I will live that long.

# 3

I'd forgotten they were there.

I'd forgotten they were there until the next day when I was lying in bed with an incredible pain in my back from the trenches I'd dug the day before. I don't know why I remembered. I just did. The pictures. The pictures.

They were hiding under my bed.

'The pictures,' I said to myself, and without even thinking, I got out of bed in the dark but slowly lightening room and got out the pictures. They were pictures of all these women I'd found in a swimwear magazine catalogue thing that came through the mail last Christmas. I'd kept it.

Back in bed I looked at the pictures of all the women with their arched backs and their smiles and their hair and lips and hips and legs and everything.

I saw the dental nurse in it – not really, of course. I just imagined her there. She would have fitted.

'God almighty,' I said when I saw one of the

women. I stared, and I felt really ashamed in my bed because . . . I don't know. It just seemed like a low thing to be doing – gawking at women first thing in the morning while everyone else in the house was still asleep. In a Christmas catalogue no less. Christmas was just under six months ago. Still, though, I stared and thumbed through the issue. Rube was still snoring his head off on the other side of the room.

The funny thing is that looking at those women is supposed to make a kid like me feel pretty good, but all it did was make me angry. I was angry that I could be so weak and stare like some sick degenerate at women who could eat me for breakfast. I thought too, but only for a second, about how a girl my age would feel looking at this stuff. It would probably make her angrier than me, because while all I wanted was to touch these women, the girl was supposed to *be* the women. This was what she was meant to aspire to. That had to be a lot of pressure.

I fell back, hopeless, to bed.

Hopeless.

'Dirty boy,' I heard Rube saying from the other day at the dentist.

'Yeah, dirty,' I agreed out loud again, and I knew

that when I got older I didn't want to be one of those sicko animal guys who had naked women from *Playboy* magazines hanging on the garage wall. I didn't want it. Right then, I didn't, so I pulled the catalogue from under my pillow and tore it in half, then quarters, and so on, knowing I would regret it. I would regret it the next time I wanted a look.

Hopeless.

When I got up I threw the pieces of women in amongst the recycling pile. I guessed they'd be back again next Christmas in a new catalogue. Glued back together. It was inevitable.

Another thing that was inevitable was that since today was Sunday I'd be going down to Lumsden Oval to watch Rube and Steve play football. Steve's side was one of the best sides around, while Rube's was one of the worst sides you would ever see in your life, Rube and his mates got flogged every week and it was always pretty brutal to watch. Rube himself wasn't too bad – him and a few others. The rest were completely useless.

Eating breakfast later on in front of *Sportsworld*, he asked me, 'So what's the bet on today's scoreline? Seventy–nil? Eighty–nil?'

'I d'know.'

'Maybe we'll finally crack the triple figures.'

'Maybe.'

We munched.

We munched as Steve came up from the basement and laid out five bananas for himself to eat. He did it every Sunday, and he ate them while grunting at Rube and me.

At the ground, Rube ended up being not too far wrong. He lost, 76–2. The other side was massive. Bigger, stronger, hairier. Rube's side only got their two points at the end of the game when the ref gave them a mercy penalty. They took the shot at goal just to get on the board. There was no sand boy or anything so the goal-kicker took his boot off, put the ball in it, and kicked the goal in just his socks. By comparison, Steve's side won a pretty good game, 24–10, and Steve, as usual, had a blinder.

All up, there were really only two halfway-interesting things about the whole day.

The first was that I saw Greg Fienni, a guy who had been my best friend until not too long ago. The thing was that we just stopped being best friends. There was no incident, no fight, no anything. We just slowly stopped being best mates. It was probably because Greg became interested in skating and he joined another gang of friends. In all honesty, he even tried to get me into the group with him, but I wasn't interested. I liked Greg a lot, but I wasn't going to follow him. He was into the skateboard culture now and I was into, well, I'm not sure what I was into. I was into roaming around on my own, and I enjoyed it.

At the ground, when I arrived, Rube's game had already started, and there was a pack of boys sitting up in the top corner, watching. When I walked past it, a voice called out to me. I knew it was Greg.

'Cam!' he called. 'Cameron Wolfe!'

'Hey.' I turned. 'How's it goin', Greg.' (I should have put a question mark there, but what I said wasn't really a question. It was a greeting.)

Next thing, Greg came out from his mates and walked over to me.

It was brief.

He asked, 'You wanna know the score?'

'Yeah, I'm a bit late, ay.' I looked strangely at his bleached, knotted hair. 'What is it?'

'Twenty–nil.'

The other side went in to score.

We laughed.

'Twenny–four.'

'Ay, sit 'own,' someone from in the group yelled out. 'Or get out of the way!'

'OK.' I shrugged, and I raised my head to Greg. I looked at his mates for a moment, then said, 'I'll see y' later, ay.' Some girls had just showed up at the group now as well. I think there were about five of them, and pretty. A couple of them were school-beauty-queen pretty while a few were that more real looking type. A realer kind of pretty. *Real girls*, I thought, *who might, if I'm lucky, talk to me someday*.

'OK.' Greg returned to his mates. 'Catch y' later.' About a month later, as it turned out.

*Funny*, I thought as I walked on, around the rope that made the field an enclosure. *Best friends once, and now we have almost nothing to say to each other*. It was interesting, how he had joined those guys and I just stayed on my own. I didn't like it or dislike it. It was just funny that things had turned out that way.

The second interesting thing was that back home, towards evening, I was sitting on our front porch watching traffic go by when Sarah and her boyfriend came walking up our street. His car was outside our house but they'd decided just to go out for a walk. The car was his pride and joy. It was a red Ford that had plenty of guts under the hood. Some people are heavily into cars, but to me they seemed pretty stupid. When you looked out my window you could see the whole city crouched under a blanket of car smog. Also, there are guys who tear up and down our street till all hours of the night and think they're absolutely brilliant.

Frankly, I think they're tossers.

Yet, who am I to say?

The first thing I do when I get up on a Sunday morning is look at pictures of half-naked women.

So.

From way down the street, I watched them: Sarah and the boyfriend. I could tell it was them because I could see Sarah's pale jeans that she wore quite often. Maybe she had a couple of pairs.

What I remember best is the way she and the boyfriend, whose name, by the way, was Bruce, were holding hands as they walked. It was nice to look at.

Even a dirty boy like me could see that.

I could.

I admitted to myself on our tiny front porch that beauty was my sister and Bruce Patterson walking up the street like that, and I honestly don't care what you call me for saying so.

In reality, that was what I wanted — what my sister and Bruce had.

Sure, I wanted those women I'd seen in that catalogue but they were just . . . not real. They were temporary. They would be like that every time — just something to pull out and then pack away.

'How's it goin'?'

'OK.'

Sarah and Bruce came onto the front porch and went inside.

Right now I still remember them walking up the road like that. I still see it.

The worst thing about it was that it didn't take a whole lot longer for Bruce to ditch Sarah for someone else. I do meet the replacement girl, later in these pages, but I only get a short look at her. Short words. Short words at a front door . . .

She seemed OK but I don't know.

I don't know anything, not really.

I—

Maybe all I know is that on that day on our front porch, when I watched Sarah and Bruce, I felt something and vowed that if I ever got a girl I would treat her right and never be bad or dirty to her or hurt her, ever. I vowed it and had all the confidence in the world that I would keep the vow.

'I'd treat her right,' I said.

'I would.'

'I would.'

'– I would.'

*I'm at the one-day cricket with a large group of guys behind me. It's raining lightly and the players are off the field, so everyone is miserable. The guys behind me have been screaming all day, abusing the opposition, each other, and anyone else they can find.*

*Earlier on, they yelled out to this guy named Harris.*

*'Oi, Harris! Show us y' bald spot!'*

*'Harris, y' dirty boy!'*

*I'm down at the fence, quiet.*

*When our mob was fielding, they gave our own players a good mouthful as well, yelling, 'Hey, Lehmann — you're lucky to be in the side — give us a wave!' He didn't, but they didn't stop. 'Hey, Lehmann, y' ignorant bloody — give us a wave or you'll get my beer on your head!'*

*After a while the guy waved and everyone cheered, but now in the rain delay, it's all getting a bit much.*

*The Mexican wave is going around the ground.*

*People go up, throwing anything they possibly can*

into the air and booing when it gets to the Members, and they don't go up like everyone else.

When the wave stops, the fellas discover a young security guard maybe twenty metres to our right. He's one of many security guards wearing black pants, black boots and yellow shirts.

He's kind of big and stupid-looking and he has black greasy hair and huge lamb-chop sideburns that go right down to his jawline.

He gets started in on: 'Hey, you! Security man! Give us a wave!'

He sees us but there's no response.

'Hey, Elvis, give us a wave!'

'Hey, Bobby Burns, give us a wave!'

He smiles and nods, very cool, and cops a barrage for it. Oohs and aahs and you're an idiot this and that.

Still they keep going.

'Hey, Travolta!'

'Hey, Travolta, give us a wave! A proper one!'

Towards the end of the dream, I suddenly feel weird and I realize that I'm actually naked.

Yes, naked.

'Geez, y' right, mate?' someone asks from behind.

Then the streaking dares start coming.

'C'mon, mate, I'll pay your fine if you make it to the other side.'

I refuse, and each time I do, another piece of clothing reappears over my skin.

The sick dream ends with me sitting there in my normal clothes again, glad and smiling that I didn't streak or do the pitch invasion I was urged to do.

As the dream suggests, I may be perverted and sick, but I'm not completely stupid.

'You won't catch me without my trousers. Not for long anyway.'

No one hears.

The players come back out.

The security guard still cops a good mouthful.

# 4

During the next week the weather turned a corner to a more intense kind of cold. The mornings at our place were pretty hectic, as always.

In her room, Sarah put her makeup on for work. Dad and Steve shouted out goodbyes. Mum cleaned up all the havoc we'd caused in the kitchen.

On the Wednesday Rube gave me a dead leg and then dragged me into the bathroom so Mum wouldn't see me writhing around in agony on the floor in our room. I laughed and whimpered at the same time as he dragged me.

'Y' don't want Mum hearin' this.' He covered my mouth. 'Remember — she tells Dad and it won't be just me who gets it. It'll be both of us.'

That was the rule at our place. If there was ever any trouble, absolutely everyone in it copped it. The old man would come down the hall with that look on him that said, *I've had one hell of a day and I didn't come home to mess around with you lot.* Then he'd pull out his back-hander – either in the ribs or across the ear. There was no mucking around. If Rube got it, I got it. So no matter how bad a fight was, it never went further than us. We were usually in enough pain as it was. The last thing we needed was Dad getting involved.

'OK, OK.' I slashed my voice at Rube once we were in the safety of the bathroom. 'Bloody, what was that for, anyway?'

'I d'know.'

'I can't believe you,' I looked up at the stupid sap. 'Ya give me a dead leg for no reason. That's shockin', that is.'

'I know.' He was grinning, and it made me push him in the bathtub and try to strangle him, but it was no use – Sarah was banging on the door.

'Get outta there!' she thumped.

'All right!'

'Now!'

'All right!'

When we were on our way to school we met some of Rube's mates.

Simon.

Jeff.

Cheese.

They were invited around in the afternoon for a game of what in our household gets called One Punch. It came about because we only have one pair of boxing gloves in our garage, so the game is pretty much a boxing match where both fighters have only the one glove. One Punch.

We played it that same Wednesday, and we were keen. Very keen. Keen to hit. Keen to get hit. Keen to get away with it, even if it meant not socializing with the rest of the family. I mean, you'd be surprised how well you can hide a bruise in the darker corner of the lounge room.

Rube's left-handed, so he likes to have the left glove. I get the right, which is my good hand. There are three rounds and the winner is declared fairly. Sometimes it's easy to tell who wins. Sometimes not.

This particular afternoon was a pretty bad one for me.

We took the gloves out into the back yard and first up was Rube against me. Rube and I always had the best fights. It was no holds barred. All it would take was one good punch from me and Rube would really try to knock my head off. One good punch from Rube on me would send the sky into my head and the clouds into my lungs. I just always tried to stay up.

So 'Ding, ding,' went Cheese with no enthusiasm, and the fight was on.

We circled the small back yard, which was half concrete, half grass. It was an urban box, not much bigger than a real boxing ring. Not much room to get out of the way. Hard concrete as well . . .

'C'mon.' Rube stepped in and went for my head, faked, and cracked my ribs. He then took a shot at my head for real and just skimmed my ear. That was when I saw him open up so I slammed one right in at his nose. It hit. Brilliant.

'*Yow!*' Simon cheered, but Rube remained focused. He walked in again without fear and didn't worry about my cocky bouncing around. He leaned in and whacked me over the eye. I blocked it and aimed up myself. He swerved me and turned me round and rammed me back against the wall, then pulled me out. He pushed me back. He hauled me onto the grass and crashed his fist into my shoulder. Yes. He hit. Oh, it was OK. It was like an axe had burst open my joint and next thing my head was rocked by his left hand. It flung forward and jammed onto my chin.

Hard.

It happened.

The sky came down.

I breathed in the clouds.

The ground wobbled.

The ground.

The ground.

I swung.

Missed.

Rube laughed, from under that increasing beard of his.

He laughed as soon as I fell down to my knees and got up a little just to crouch there. The count came, with delight. Rube: 'One – two – three—'

Once I was up again and the cheers of Simon, Jeff and Cheese were no longer mere blurs, there were only a few more punches and Round One was over.

I sat in the corner of the yard, in the shade.

Round Two.

It was much the same, only this time Rube went down once as well.

Round Three was a dog fight.

Both of us came out throwing hard and I recall reefing at Rube's ribs close to seven or eight times and copping at least three good shots on my cheekbone. It was brutal. The neighbour on our left kept caged parrots and had a midget dog. The birds screeched from over the fence and the midget dog barked and jumped at the fence while my brother and I fought each other senseless. His fist was this big brown blur that kept driving forward from his long arm, pumping out at me and singing as it pushed my skin into my bones. All was mirrored and shaky and shivery and getting orange-dark and I could feel that metallic taste of blood crawling from my nose to my lip, over my teeth and onto my tongue. Or was I bleeding inside my mouth? I didn't know. I didn't know anything until I was crouched down again and dizzy and feeling like I might throw up.

'One – two—'

The count meant nothing this time.

I ignored it.

All I did this time was sit down against the back fence till I recovered.

'Y' OK?' Rube asked a bit later, his rough hair swinging down into his eyes.

I nodded.

I was.

Back inside, I surveyed the damage and it didn't look too good.

There was no blood in my nose. It did turn out to

be in my mouth, and I had a black eye. A good one. No hiding it. Not today. No point. Mum was going to kill us.

She did.

She took one look at me and said, 'And what happened to you?'

'Ah, nothin'.'

Then she saw Rube, who had a slightly swollen lip.

'Ah, you boys.' She shook her head. 'You disgust me, I swear it. Can you not go one week without hurting each other?'

No, we couldn't.

We were always hurting each other, whether it was boxing, or playing football in the lounge room with a rolled-up pair of socks.

'Well, stay apart for a while,' she ordered us, and we obeyed the order. We tried hard to listen to our mother because she was tough and she cleaned rich people's houses for a living and she worked hard to let us have an OK house. We didn't like it much when she was disappointed in us.

The disappointment was to continue.

It really got bad throughout the next day because some of my teachers became a bit concerned about the state of my face and the way that every second week it seemed to have a bruise or a scab or a graze on it. They asked me all these weird questions about how things were at home and how I got on with my parents and all that kind of thing. I just told them I got on pretty well with everyone and that things were just as usual at home. Pretty good.

'Are you sure?' they asked. As if I'd lie. Maybe I should have told them I ran into the door or fell down the basement stairs. That would have been a laugh. Mainly I just told them that I did boxing as a recreational sport and that I hadn't really become too good at it yet.

They clearly didn't believe what I told them because on Thursday afternoon my mother got a call from the school, requesting a meeting with the principal and the head of welfare.

She came on Friday at lunch and made sure Rube and I were there as well.

Outside, just before she went into that welfare office, she said, 'Wait here and don't move till I say you can come in.' We nodded and sat down, and after about ten minutes, she opened the door and said, 'Right – in.' We got up and went in.

Inside the office, the principal and the welfare officer stared at us with a kind of amused, measured repugnance. So did Mum, for that matter, and the reason for this became quite clear when she reached into her handbag and pulled out our boxing gloves and said happily, 'OK, put them on.'

'Ah, c'mon, Mum,' Rube protested.

'No no no,' insisted Mr Dennison, the principal. 'We're very interested in seeing this.'

'Come on, boys,' my mother egged us on. 'Don't be ashamed . . .' But that was the whole point. Embarrass us. Humiliate us. Shame us. It wasn't hard to see what was going on, as each of us put our glove on.

'My sons,' my mother said to the principal, and then to us. 'My sons.'

The look on our mother's face was one of bitter disappointment. She looked ready to cry. The wrinkles around her eyes were dark-dry riverbeds, waiting. No water came. She just looked. Away. Then, with purpose, she looked at us and seemed ready to spit at our shoes and disown us. I didn't blame her.

'So this is what they do,' she told them. 'I'm sorry about all this, to waste your time like this.'

'It's OK,' Dennison told her, and she shook hands with both him and the welfare woman.

'I'm sorry,' she said again and walked out, not even looking at us again. She left us standing there, wearing those gloves, like two ridiculous beasts in winter.

Don't ask me why, but I'm in Russia, sitting on a bus in Moscow.

It's crowded.

The bus moves slowly.

It's freezing.

The guy next to me has the window seat and he's holding some kind of rodent that hisses at me even if I so much as look at it. The guy nudges me, says something, and laughs. When I ask him if this really is Moscow (because of course I've never been there), he starts having this long drawn-out conversation with me, which is a miracle because I can't even say a word to him on account of not knowing the language.

He's unbelievable.

Talking.

Laughing, and by the end of it, I actually like the guy. I laugh at all his jokes by the lines they make on his face.

'Slow bus,' I say, but of course he has no idea.

Russia.

*Can you tell me what in God's name I'm doing in Russia?*

*The bus is freezing as well — did I mention that already? Yeah? Well, trust me, it is, and all the windows are fogged up.*

*Shiver.*

*I shiver in my seat until I can take it no longer.*

*Stand.*

*I try to get up but I seem pasted down. It's like I've actually been frozen to the seat.*

*'Get up,' I tell myself, but I can't. I can't!*

*Then I see someone amongst the crowd in the aisle hobbling towards me.*

*No.*

*Oh, no.*

*It's an old woman, and since being in Russia, I've realized that these old women really get into the thick of it. And worse still, she's looking right at me. Right, at me.*

*'Help me up,' I say to the guy next to me. I beg, but he does nothing. He even turns away to sleep, squashing his rodent up against the window. It gags.*

*She's still coming.*

*No.*

*A nightmare.*

*She grimaces and fixes her eyes on mine, silently telling me to get out of the seat.*

Get up! *I shriek inside me.*

*I can't, and she —*

*Arrives.*

'Yah!' she begins, and from there, there is no stopping her. She spits her Russian swearing right in my face and gives me a barrage with her fists. Her tiny ferocious hands try to lift me by my clothes to throw me from the seat.

'I'm sorry!' I wail, but this old lady is like fury personified, sending flurries all over me.

Later, I'm sitting down in the aisle, with the seat of my pants still stuck on the seat. A middle-aged man who speaks English tells me, 'Shouldn't offend the lady, old boy.'

'No kidding,' I agree, trying to keep my bare skin off the frozen floor.

The old lady smiles down at me, with disgust.

# 5

This is an important chapter.

I think so, anyway.

The bruises on my face healed pretty quickly and I spent the next while of my life just hanging around. A happening was looming. It was out there somewhere beyond the regular enclosed life that I had been living. It was out there, not waiting, but existing. Being. Perhaps it was only slightly wondering if I would come to it.

Maybe I'm just talking stupid.

Anyway.

The happening that happened was that I met this girl when I was working with Dad on a Saturday.

She was something, I promise you.

I'd spent the whole morning digging a trench under the house at this job in a district maybe five kilometres away from ours, and I was dead. Dead by lunch.

There was dirt all over me and my neck was

straightened and stiffened from bending over and digging. When I came out from underneath, she was there. She was there with her mother and father and she was so real I nearly choked on the nothingness in my mouth. My height, she was, and calm and real in the face. She smiled at me with real lips and her real voice said 'Hi' when we met.

I wiped my right hand on my pants and shook all their hands. Mother. Father. Girl.

'My son, Cameron,' my dad told them when I crawled out, shaking the dirt from my hair. He even sounded like he remotely liked having me around.

'G'day,' I said when I faced up to them, and Dad kind of took the parents on a tour of what we'd done on their property. They were having pretty massive extensions done, which were cramping up the yard a little. It was a nice house, though.

The girl.

'Rebecca,' her mother had told me.

When Dad was doing the grand tour I was alone with her.

What was I meant to do?

Talk?

Wait?

Sit down?

All up, all we did was stand there a while and then sit on these deck chair sort of things. I looked away and looked at her and looked away again.

What an animal.

I sure had a way with the ladies, didn't I?

Finally, when it was almost too late and the old fellas were coming back, I said to her in this crazed quiet voice, 'I like workin' here,' and after the silence, we both laughed a bit and I thought, *What a weird thing to say*. I like working here. I like working here. I Like. Working here. I Like working here.

As I repeated it over in my head I wondered if she knew what it really meant.

I think she did.

Rebecca.

It was a nice name, and while I liked the calmness in her face, I liked her voice better. I remembered it and let it chant across me. Just that 'Hi.' Pathetic, I know, but when your experience with women is as minimal as mine, you take whatever you can get.

All afternoon, it lasted. There was even very little pain in the work I did because I had Rebecca now. I had her voice and the realness of it to numb everything. It numbed the blisters forming at the base of my fingers and blunted the blade seeking my spine.

'Hi,' she'd said. 'Hi,' and she'd laughed with me when I said something stupid. I'd been laughed at before by girls, but it was rare for me to laugh *with* one. It was rare to feel OK with a city over my shoulder and a girl's face so close to mine. She had breath and sight and she was real. That was the best thing. She was realer than the dental nurse because she wasn't behind a counter being paid to be friendly. And she was definitely realer than the women in that catalogue thing because there was no way I would ever tear this girl up. There was no way I would dare to hurt her or curse her or hide her under my bed.

Eyes. Alive eyes. Light hair falling down her back. A pimple at the side of her face, near her hairline. Nice neck, shoulders. Not a beauty queen. Not one of those. You know the ones.

She was real.

She played music later on and it wasn't anything much that I liked, but that made her realer still. The whole situation even made me smile at Dad when he told me off for digging something in the wrong place.

'I'm sorry, Dad,' I said.

'Dig over there.'

I wonder if he knew. I doubt it. He didn't seem

to catch on when I asked if we'd be back here next week.

'Yeah, we'll be back,' he'd answered bluntly.

'Good,' but I said it only to me.

A bit later, I asked, 'What's these people's last name?'

'Conlon.'

Rebecca Conlon.

The thing that hit me most was that I suddenly started praying. I started saying these prayers for Rebecca Conlon and her family. I couldn't stop myself.

'Please bless Rebecca Conlon,' I kept saying to God. 'Just let her be OK, OK? Let her and her family be OK tonight. That's all I ask. In the name of the Father, the Son, and the Holy Spirit,' and I crossed myself like the Catholics do and I'm not even a Catholic. I don't know what I am.

During the next week, I kept praying, and I kept making sure to remember her face, and her voice.

'I'd be good to her,' I kept telling God. 'I would.'

I was actually torn between the love I had for her face and her body and the love I had for her voice. Her face had character all right. Strength. I loved it. I definitely loved her neck and her throat and her shoulders and her arms and legs. All of it – and then there was the voice.

The voice came from somewhere in her. It came from somewhere that didn't show itself, I hoped, to just anyone.

The question was, *Which part of her was I interested in most?* Was it the look of her, or the inner realness I could sense slipping out?

I started taking walks, just to think of her – just to imagine what she was doing and if by any chance she was thinking of me.

It became torture.

'God, is she thinking of me?' I asked God.

God didn't answer so I just didn't know. All I knew was that I walked parallel to urban traffic that laughed as it went past me. Crowds of people dropped out of buses and trains and ignored me as they went past. I didn't care. I had Rebecca Conlon. Nothing else meant a whole lot. Even back home when I bickered with Rube I didn't worry. I just kept not worrying, because she was somewhere near it all in my thoughts.

Joy.

Is that what I felt?

Sometimes.

At other times I was shouldered by thoughts of doubt and a kind of truth that told me she hadn't thought of me at all. It was possible, because things never work out how they should. It was most likely that a sweet girl like that could do a whole lot better than me. She could do better than a fella who plotted ridiculous robberies with his brother, got thrown out of newsagents', and humiliated his mother.

Sometimes I thought about her naked, but never for long. I didn't want her only like that. Honestly.

I wanted to find the place where her voice came from. That was what I wanted. I wanted to be nice to her. I wanted to please her, and I begged for it to happen. Begging gets you nowhere, though. I knew that was true, but I did it inside me anyway as I counted the hours till I was going back to her.

Things happened during the week that will follow in the next chapters, but now I should tell you at the end of this one here what happened when Dad and I showed up at the Conlons' the next Saturday.

This is what happened.

My heart beat big.

*   *   *

*One of them's back.*

*Can you believe it?*

*The nerve of her.*

*Do you know who I mean? It's one of the women from that swimwear catalogue, and she comes to me in our kitchen.*

*Seductively.*

*It's musty and half dark. Sweaty.*

*'Hello, Cameron.' She keeps coming, and she pulls a chair over to sit right opposite me. Our knees touch — that's how close she comes to me. Her smile is one of definite something. Danger? Lust? Eroticism?*

*How can I dream this now?*

*Tonight?*

*After what's been happening lately?*

*I've gotta be kidding me.*

*Is this a test?*

*Well, whatever it is, she leans closer and licks her lips. Her swimsuit is a bikini and it's yellow and it shows a whole lot of her. Can you believe this? She lets one of her fingers touch my neck and she strokes her way down with it, and her fingernail is just light enough not to scratch. It's smooth, and something tells me to make the most of it, to never let her stop. Then something else screams silently somewhere in my feet that I must tell her to stop. It rises.*

She's on me.

Breathing.

I smell her perfume and feel the soft thrill of her hair.

Her hands undress me and her mouth takes me.

I feel it.

Gathering.

Pushing.

Against me.

She falls, letting her teeth touch the skin of my throat.

She kisses, long, with her tongue touching—

I jump.

'What?'

I'm standing.

'What?' she asks. Ohh . . .

'I can't.' I hold her hand to tell her the truth. 'I can't. I just can't.'

'Why not?'

Her eyes are fire-blue and I almost allow her to go on as she begins stroking my stomach and searching for the rest of me. I stop her, just in time, and I wonder how I do it.

I turn away and answer her.

'I've got someone real. Someone who isn't just—'

'Just what?'

Truth: 'Something I only lust for.'

'Is that all I am? A thing?'

'Yes,' and I see her change. She is ghost-like, and when I reach out to touch her, my hand goes through. 'See,' I explain, 'look at me. A guy like me can't really touch someone like you. It's just the way it is.'

When she disappears completely, I understand that my reality isn't the catalogue girl or school beauty queen or anyone like that. My reality is the real girl on her left.

On the table, the swimsuit model has left her purse. I go to pick it up, but I don't open it for fear of it blowing up in my face.

The beauty queen, I long for.

The real girl, I long to please.

Dream complete.

# 6

Remember when I said how I liked watching Sarah and Bruce come up the street that Sunday night?

Well, during the week that all seemed to change.

There was also another change, because Steve, who normally didn't get home from his office job until about eight at night, was home too. The reason for this was that the previous day at football, he'd turned on his ankle. It was nothing serious, he'd said, but on the Monday morning, his ankle was the size of a shot-put ball. The doctor had ruled him out for six weeks because of ligament damage.

'But I'll be back in a month, you watch.'

He sat on the floor with his foot raised on some pillows and his crutches next to him. He would be stranded at home for a fortnight, after his boss gave him half of his holiday early. This drove Steve mad, not only because he would miss some of his holiday in the summer, but because he hated just sitting around.

His sombre mood sure didn't help things in the lounge room between Sarah and Bruce.

On the couch on Tuesday, rather than going at it like they normally did, they both seemed to be glued down by tension.

'Smell this pillow,' Rube instructed me at one point as I watched them while trying not to.

'Why?'

'It stinks.'

'I don't feel like smellin' it.'

'Go on.' His hairy, threatening face came closer and I knew he wouldn't take no for an answer.

He threw the pillow over and I was expected to pick it up and stuff it in my face and tell him if it stank. Rube was always making me do things like that – things that seemed ridiculous and meaningless.

'Go on!'

'All right!'

'Go sniff it,' he said, 'and tell me it doesn't smell like Steve's pyjamas.'

'Steve's pyjamas?'

'Yeah,'

'My pyjamas don't stink.' Steve glared.

'Mine do,' I said. It was a joke. No one laughed. So I turned back to Rube.

'How do *you* know what Steve's pyjamas smell like? You go round sniffin' people's pyjamas? Are you a bloody pyjama-sniffer or somethin'?'

Rube eyed me, unimpressed. 'Y' can smell 'em when he walks past. Now *sniff*!'

I did it and conceded that the pillow didn't smell like roses.

'I told ya.'

'Great.'

I returned it to him and he threw it back where it was. That was Rube. The pillow stank and he knew it stank and was concerned about it. He wanted to talk about it, but one thing was certain – there was no way he would wash it. Back in the corner of the couch, the pillow sat, stinking. I could still smell it now, but only because Rube had brought it up. It was probably my imagination. Thanks, Rube.

What made things even more uncomfortable was the fact that normally, if Bruce and Sarah weren't all over each other, they would at least throw something into the conversation, no matter how stupid we were talking. On that day, however, Bruce said nothing, and Sarah said nothing. They only sat there and watched the movie they'd rented. Not one word.

While all this was going on, I'd better point out

that I was praying for Rebecca Conlon and her family. It led me to even start praying for my own family. I prayed that I wouldn't let Mum down any more and that Dad wouldn't work so hard that he'd kill himself before he hit forty-five. I prayed for Steve's ankle to get better. I prayed that Rube would make something of himself sometime. I prayed that Sarah was OK right there and then and that she and Bruce would be OK. Just be OK. *Be OK.* I said that a lot. I said it as I started praying for the whole stupid human race and for anyone who was hurting or hungry or dying or being raped at that exact moment in time.

*Just let 'em be OK,* I asked God. *All those people with AIDS and all that stuff as well. Just let 'em be OK right now, and those homeless blokes with beards and rags and cut-up shoes and rotten teeth. Let 'em be OK . . . But mainly, let Rebecca Conlon be OK.*

It was starting to drive me crazy.

Really.

When Sarah and Bruce weren't aware I was watching them, I stared at them hard and wondered how just days and weeks ago they were all over each other.

I wondered how this could happen.

It scared me.

*God, please bless Rebecca Conlon. Let her be OK . . .*

How could things be so different all of a sudden?

Later on, when I was back in Rube's and my room, I could hear the drone of Sarah and Bruce talking behind the wall, in her room. The city was dark except for the building lights that seemed to appear like sores — like Band-Aids had been ripped off to expose the city's skin.

The only thing that seemed never to change was the city at this transition time between afternoon and evening. It always became murky and aloof and ignorant of what was going on. There were thousands of households throughout that city and there was something happening in all of them. There was some kind of story in each, but self contained. No one else knew. No one else cared. No one else knew about Sarah Wolfe and Bruce Patterson, or cared about Steven Wolfe's ankle. No one else out there prayed for them or prayed repeatedly for Rebecca Conlon. No one.

So I saw that there was only me. There was only me who could worry about what was happening here, inside these walls of my life. Other people had their own worlds to worry about, and in the end, they had to fend for themselves, just like us.

By the time I went to bed, I was going in circles.

Praying.

Worrying about Sarah.

Praying like an incoherent fool.

I could feel the city at the window, but mostly, I remained in my head, hearing every thought – quiet but loud, and true.


*The future:*

*Time to relax.*

*We're at the edge of the city, right next to it, as if we can reach across and touch the buildings – reach in and turn off the lights that try shining in our eyes to blind us.*

*We're fishing, Rube and I.*

*We've never fished before, but we are today, through this whole evening.*

*Our lines dangle in what is a huge, darkening blue lake with stars dropping up through the water.*

*The water is still, but alive. We can feel it moving beneath the old beat-up boat we have hired from some con man on the shore. Once in a while it shifts beneath us. We are unafraid, at first, because although nothing has been totally stable, we know where we are, and things aren't moving along too rapidly.*

*We catch.*

*Nothing.*

*Absolutely. Nothing.*

'Bloody hopeless.' *Rube initiates conversation.*

'I told y' we shouldn't have gone fishing. Who knows what's in this lake?'

'Dead souls from the city.' *Rube smiles with a kind of sarcastic joy.* 'What'll we do if we get one on the end of our line?'

'Jump ship, mate.'

'Too bloody right.'

*The water moves again, and slowly, waves start rolling in from somewhere we can't see. They rise up and jump into the boat, and they get higher.*

*There's a smell.*

'A smell?'

'Yeah, can't you smell it?' *I ask Rube. I say it like an accusation.*

'I can, yeah, now that you mention it.'

*The water is excessively high now, lifting the boat and us and throwing us back down. A wave hits my face and I get a mouthful. The taste, it's grotesque, burning, and I can tell by the look on Rube's face that he's swallowed some too.*

'It's petrol,' *he tells me.*

'Oh God.'

The waves die a little now, and I turn to a boat that sits closer to the city, right near the shore. There's a guy in it, and a girl. The guy steps out onto the shore with something in his hand.

It – glows.

'No!' I stand and throw my arms out.

He does it. Cigarette.

He does it as I see another person doing laps across the bay, intense. Who is it? I wonder, and in another boat still, a man and a woman are also rowing, middle-aged.

The guy throws his cigarette into the lake.

Red and yellow rolls into my eyes.

Oblivion.

# 7

On the Thursday of that week, Rube also conned me into making a new exodus — a journey away from our normal robbery expeditions.

Street signs.

That was the new plan.

It was still afternoon when he thought about it and told me which sign he wanted to get.

'The give-way,' he said. 'Down Marshall Street.' He smiled. 'We sneak out, right, say elevenish, with one of Dad's spanners — the one you can adjust by rubbing that thing on the top . . .'

'The wrench?'

'Yeah, that's it . . . We put our hoods on, walk down there casual as M. E. Waugh in bat, I climb up on your shoulders, and we take the sign.'

'What for?'

'What, exactly, do you mean, *what for*?'

'I mean, what's the point?'

'Point?' He was, what's the word? Exasperated.

Frustrated. 'We don't need a point, son. We're juvenile, we're dirty, we don't have girls, we have noses full of snot, throats sore as hell, we've got scabs on us, we suffer bouts of acne, we've got no girls – did I already say that? – little money, we eat mushrooms mashed next to meat almost every night for dinner and drown 'em in tomato sauce so we can't taste 'em. What more reasons do we need?' My brother threw his head back on his bed and stared desperately at the ceiling. 'We don't ask for much, dear God! You know that!'

So that was it.

The next mission.

I swear it, that night, we were like savages, just as Rube had described in his outburst. It shocked me at first that he knew us like that. Like I did. Only, Rube was proud of it.

Maybe we didn't know *who* we were, but we knew *what* we were, and to Rube it made acts of vandalism such as stealing street signs seem like a logical thing to do. He sure didn't feel like considering that we could end up in a police cell without the proper safety-standard bars.

Of course, we knew we couldn't succeed.

The only problem was, we did.

We snuck out the back door of home at about quarter to twelve with our hoods hunching over our heads and footsteps raking us forward. We walked calmly, even toughly, down our street with smoky breath, hands in pockets, and whispers of greatness stuffed down our socks. Our sniffs and breathing scratched us through the air, pulling it apart, and I felt like that Julius Caesar guy going to conquer another empire – and all we were doing was stealing a lousy grey-and-pink triangle that should have been white and red.

Give way.

'More like give *away*,' Rube snickered as we arrived at the scene of the sign. He got up, slipped, then got up again on my shoulders.

'Right.' He spoke again once he found balance. 'Spanner.'

'Huh?'

'*Spanner*, you stupid sap.' His whisper was harsh and heavily smoked in the cold.

'Oh, right, yeah, I forgot.'

I handed him the spanner or wrench or whatever you want to call it and my brother proceeded to unscrew the give-way sign on the junction of Marshall and Carlisle streets.

'Geez, she's a bit bloody stubborn,' Rube pointed out. 'The bolt's so rusty that all the garbage is gettin' stuck on the nut. Just keep holdin' me up, OK?'

'I'm gettin' tired,' I mentioned.

'Well, get through it. The pain barrier. The pain barrier, son. All the greats could always break through the pain barrier.'

'The great whats? Sign stealers?'

'No.' It was sharp. 'Athletes, you yobbo.'

Then came the triumph.

'Right,' Rube announced, 'I've got it.' He jumped off my shoulders with the sign just as a light came on in one of the dilapidated flats on the corner.

A woman stepped out onto her balcony and sighed, 'Ah, grow up, will y's.'

'C'mon.' Rube tugged at my sweatshirt. 'Go go go!'

We took off, laughing as Rube held the sign up above his head, cheering, 'Oh, yes!'

Even when we snuck back into our house, the adrenaline was still crouching in my blood, then springing forward, taking off. It disappeared slowly when we were back in our bedroom. With the light off in our room almost instantly, Rube slid the sign

under his bed and said, just for fun, 'Tell Mum or
Dad about this and I'll see if I can fit this sign down
your throat.' I laughed a little and soon fell asleep,
still hearing the gentle sounds of women sighing at
undesirables in the middle of the night. I wondered
about Rebecca Conlon before sleep came as well, and
I remembered moments when we walked down the
street and when we were abducting the sign in which
I pretended she was watching me. I wasn't sure if she
would like me or think I was a complete idiot.
Complete idiot, most likely.

'Ah, well,' I whispered to myself under my
blanket. 'Ah, well,' and I started praying for her and
everyone else I had prayed for lately. In the night,
not long after sleep captured me, my dream came –
a bad one. A nightmare. A proper one.

You will see it soon enough . . .

Next day, in the morning, Rube took the sign out
to admire it again in the comfort of our room. I was
coming back in from the shower.

'Isn't she beautiful?' he told me.

'Yeah.' I didn't sound too keen, though.

'What's with you?'

'Nothin'.' It was the nightmare.

'OK.' He put the sign away again and poked his

head into the hall. 'Aah.' He looked back at me. 'Y' left the bathroom door open again – do you do that on purpose just to let the cold in before I go in the shower?'

'I forgot.'

'Well lift your game.'

He left, but I followed him, with my hair wet and sticking up in all directions.

'Where the hell do y' think you're going?'

'I've gotta tell you something.'

'Right.' He shut me out of the bathroom. I heard the shower go on, the door unlock, the curtain shut, and then a shout came. 'Come in!'

I went in and sat on the shut-up toilet.

'Well,' he called out to me, 'what is it?'

I began talking about the nightmare I'd had, and through the heat in the bathroom, an extra heat seemed to come from out of me, overpowering it. I took a minute or two to explain the dream properly.

When I finished, all Rube said was, 'So what?' The steam was getting intense.

'So what should we do?'

The shower stopped.

Rube stuck his head round the curtain.

'Pass me that towel.'

I did it.

He dried himself and stepped out, breaking through the steam with, 'Well, it's certainly a disturbing dream you speak of, son.'

He had no idea how disturbing. It was me who dreamed it. It was me who had believed it when it was in me. It was me who.

End.

End this.

No . . .

It was me who had woken up in the darkness of our triumph with sweat eating my eyes out, and a silent scream pressed down on my lips.

In the bathroom now, I suggested, 'We've gotta take the sign back.'

Rube had other ideas, at first.

He came closer and said, 'We can ring the RTA and tell 'em the sign needs replacing.'

'It'll take absolute weeks for *them* to replace it.'

Rube paused, then said, 'Yeah, good thinkin'.' Unhappiness. 'The state of our roads down this way is a disgrace to the nation.'

'So what do we do?' I asked again. I was genuinely concerned now, for the safety of the public at large, and I also remembered a story I'd seen on the news a year or so back where these guys in America got something like twenty years for stealing a stop sign because it caused a fatal accident. Look it up if you don't believe me. It happened.

'What do we do?' I asked again.

Rube answered by not answering quickly.

He walked out of the bathroom, got dressed, and then held his head in his hands as he sat on my bed.

'What else *can* we do?' he asked, almost pleaded. 'We take it back. I s'pose.'

'Really?'

Savages, all right.

Savages, frightened.

'Yeah.' He was miserable. 'Yes. We take it back.' It was as if Rube himself had been robbed of something — but what? Why this need to take things? Was it just to feel how it felt to cut up the rules and feel good about being bad? Maybe it was that Rube felt like a failure and he was proving it to himself by trying to steal. Maybe he wanted to be like the hero in the American movies we see on TV. Frankly, I had no idea what was going on in his head and that was that.

Before we went to school, he pulled the sign

out and gave it one last sad, adoring stare.

That night, Friday night, we took it back at around eleven and nobody caught us, thank God. It would have been pretty ironic — busted for stealing a sign when we were actually returning it.

'Well,' he said when we got home, 'we're back, empty-handed. As usual.'

'Mm.' I couldn't get a word out just then.

One thing I will always remember about that night now is that when we made it back home, Steve was sitting out on the front porch in the cold. His crutches were still next to him, because his ankle was still very screwed up. He sat there, on our old couch, with a mug perched up on the railing.

When we slipped down the side of the house, sort of ignoring him, I heard his voice.

I returned.

I asked.

'What did you just say?' I said it just very normally, like I was interested in what he'd said.

He repeated.

This: 'I can't believe we're brothers.'

He shook his head.

He spoke again.

'You guys are such losers.'

To tell you the truth, it was the vacancy he'd said it with that chewed into me. He said it like we were so far below him that he could barely be bothered. Then, considering what we had just done, I could almost see his point of view. How could Steven Wolfe be of the same blood as Rube and me, and even Sarah for that matter?

All the same, I only stopped slightly before walking off, hearing a high-pitched noise cut open my head, from inside. It whined, as if injured.

Back in our room, I asked Rube where he would have put the sign on the wall in our room. Maybe I asked it to forget what Steve had said to me.

'Here?'

'Nah.'

'Here?'

'Nah.'

'Here?'

I didn't get an answer for a long time, and that night the light was left on for a while as Rube thought thoughts about things I would never know. All he did was lie on his bed, softly rubbing his beard, as though it was all he had left.

Once settled on top of my own bed, I thought intensely about the next day, working at the

Conlons'. Rebecca Conlon. I'd thought the day would never come, but the next day, I was going back. Once I forgot about Rube and Steve, it was beautiful to be alive, conscience free and awaiting a girl who was worth praying for.

After a long while, Rube made a statement.

He said, 'Cameron. I wouldn't have put that sign anywhere on our wall.'

I turned to look at him. 'Why not?'

'You know why not.' He continued staring towards the ceiling. Only his mouth moved. 'Because the moment Mum saw it, she would have killed me.'

*There's a car, prowling around the city. It's orange and big, and it makes the heavy, brooding sound cars like that make. It roars around the streets, though it always stops at red lights, stop signs, and all that kind of thing.*

*Cut to somewhere else —*

*Rube and I are walking, out of our front gate, supposedly to watch Steve play football, even though it's about two o'clock in the morning. It's cold. You know, that kind of sickly cold. Cold that somehow breathes. It ploughs into our mouths, blunt and hurtful.*

*A question.*

*Rube: 'You ever think about beatin' up the old man?'*

'Our old man?'

'Sure.'

'Why?'

'I don't know — don't you reckon it'd be fun?'

'No, I don't.'

At that, we return to silence, walking. Our feet drag over the path as a few stray cars stroll by. Taxis come past and swerve all over the road, a garbage truck struggles past us, overweight. The orange car rolls past, growling.

'Tossers,' I say to Rube.

'Definitely.'

As he says it, the car takes off and we hear it draw away, then come back on a side street behind us.

Cut to somewhere else —

Rube and I are standing at the corner of Marshall and Carlisle streets. Rube crouches down as the closing statements of a car call closer. He crouches down, holding the give-way sign we stole between his legs. The pole there is empty when I look at it. It's just an empty pole embedded in cement.

Arrival.

The orange car comes up Marshall Street, almost devouring its own speed, gathering it greedily.

When it gets to us it's flying.

No sign.

No sign.

It speeds past us, and as my eyes smash shut, there is an almighty clenching sound of metal wrapping into metal, a shriek, and a delayed downpour of broken glass.

Rube crouches.

I stand, eyes still shut.

Murmuring silence.

It's everywhere.

My eyes open and we walk.

Rube drops the sign, stands, and we walk in a slow, shuddering panic down to the cars that look to have bitten into each other in attack.

Inside, the people look swallowed.

They are dead and bleeding and mangled.

They're dead.

'They're dead!' I call across to Rube, but nothing comes out of my mouth. No sound. No voice.

Then a dead body comes to life.

The eyes in it punch out at me and when the person cries out, the sound in my ears is unbearable. It sends me to the ground, squashing my hands to the side of my head.

# 8

When I went to the Conlons' place the next morning with Dad, it's true, my heart beat so hard, or big, as I originally put it, that it kind of hurt. It pumped something into my throat, causing me to salivate, with questions.

What would I say?

How would I act when I saw her?

Nice?

Calm?

Indifferent?

That shy and sensitive style that had never worked for me in the past?

I had no idea.

In the van on the way over, I thought I was going to choke or suffocate or something. Such was the feeling this girl had planted inside me. It grew as we drove closer to her house. It even got to the point where I was hoping the next light would be red so I had more time to think things through. It's funny.

I had all week to go over this, to be prepared, and now Saturday had come and I was at a loss. Maybe I'd had too much time to think about it. Maybe I should have spent less time worrying about Sarah and Bruce, and Steve, and stealing and returning road signs with Rube. Maybe then my own game wouldn't have suffered. Maybe then I would have been all right.

If.

Only.

It was no use.

All was lost.

*When we arrive there*, I thought, *I'd be better off just sticking my head into the ditch and digging a hole for myself.* Girls didn't go for someone like me. What self-respecting girl could even stomach me? Permanently messy hair. Grubby hands and feet. Uneven smile. Uneasy, limping walk. No, this was definitely no good. Not at all.

*Let's face it*, I even lectured myself inside, *you don't even deserve a girl.* I was right. I didn't. I showed clear signs of dubious morality, at best. I was easily led by my brother. I committed pathetic acts that were petty and done just for some kind of wild pride that was so ridiculous it was hard to comprehend. All I was was a panting desperate mess of a person, scrambling around for something to make me OK . . .

Then. Suddenly.

In an instant, I thought how strange it was that I never prayed for myself. Was I unable to be saved? Was I so dirty that I didn't deserve a prayer? Perhaps. Maybe.

Yet, *I did get Rube to return the sign*, I managed to rationalize. *So maybe I'm not so bad after all*. That was better — a bit of positive thought, as Dad's panel van rumbled on in the direction of my fate.

When we pulled up at the house, I even started to have some tiny moments of belief that maybe I wasn't the ugly, sick degenerate I'd judged myself to be. I started telling myself that I was probably quite normal. I remembered what I thought that day back in the dental surgery — that all young boys are pretty disgusting, like beasts. Maybe the challenge was to somehow rise above it. Maybe that's what I was looking for with Rebecca Conlon. Just one chance to prove that I could be nice and respectable instead of purely lustful and terrible. I just wanted one shot to treat her right and I knew I wouldn't blow it.

I couldn't.

I wouldn't allow myself.

'I'm not gonna blow it,' I whispered to myself as I got out of the van. I took a big breath, like I was walking towards the most important thing in my life. Then I realized. This *was* the most important thing in my life.

'Take this,' my father told me, handing me a shovel, and through the morning, I worked hard and waited for Rebecca Conlon to make her appearance. Then I found out in a conversation between Dad and her mother that she wasn't there. She'd slept the night at a friend's place.

'Brilliant,' I said, in the gap between my tongue and my throat.

And do you know what the worst part of it was?

It was knowing that if Rebecca Conlon was coming to work at my place, I would have made sure without doubt that I was there to see her. I would have been there. I would have nailed myself to the floor two days earlier if I knew she was coming, just to make sure I wouldn't miss her.

'I would have,' I said, agreeing with myself, as I kept working.

I worked myself into a state of numbness. It was awful. Even Dad asked if I was OK. I told him yes, but we both knew I was miserable.

At the end of the day, when the girl still hadn't arrived, Dad gave me an extra ten dollars. He gave it to me and said, 'You did well today, boy.' Then he walked away and stopped, turned, and said, 'I mean, Cameron.'

'Thanks,' I said, and even though I tried so hard to make it real, the smile I gave my father was one of misery.

'I'd have treated her well,' I said to the city outside my window back home, but it was no use. The city didn't care, and in the next room, Sarah and Bruce were arguing.

Rube came in and slumped forward onto his bed. He put his pillow over his head and said, 'I think I liked 'em better when they were all over each other.'

'Yeah, me too.'

I too slumped onto my bed, only I decided to turn on my back and cover my eyes with my hands. Squashing my thumbs in, I made myself see patterns in my darkness.

'What's for dinner?' I asked Rube, dreading the answer.

'Sausages, I think, and leftover mushrooms.'

'Ah, beautiful.' I turned on my side, in pain. 'Just bloody beautiful.'

Rube took his pillow off his head then and gravely said, 'We're out of tomato sauce as well.'

'Even more beautiful.'

I stopped speaking then, but I continued moaning inside. After a while I got tired of it and thought, *Don't worry, Cameron. Every dog will have his day.*

Just, not on this day.

(We did eat the mushrooms, by the way. We looked down at them, then up. Then down again. Disgusting. No point backing away. We ate them because we were us and in the end, we ate everything. We always did. We always ate everything. Even if we spewed up our dinner and had it given to us again the next night, Rube and I probably would have eaten that too.)

*There's a big crowd, around a fight, and they are all yelling and howling and screaming, as though punches are landing and fists are moulding faces. It's a huge crowd, about eight deep, so it is very difficult to push my way through.*

*I get down on my knees.*

*I crawl.*

*I look for gaps and then slip through them, until eventual-
ly, I'm there. I'm at the front of the crowd, which
is a giant circle, thick.*

*'Go!' the guy next to me yells. 'Go hard!'*

*Still, I look at the crowd. I don't watch the fight. Not
yet.*

*There are all kinds of people amongst this crowd.
Skinny. Fat. Black. White. Yellow. They all look on and
scream into the middle of the ring.*

*The guy next to me is always shrieking in my ear,
drilling right through my skull to my brain. I feel his voice
in my lungs. That's how loud he is. Nothing stops him,
even the ones behind who throw words at him to make him
shut up. It is no use.*

*I try stopping him myself, by asking him something — a
shout over the rest of the crowd. 'Who y' going for?' I ask.*

*He stops his noise. Immediately.*

*He stares.*

*At the fight. Then at me.*

*A few more seconds pass and he says, 'I'm goin' for the
underdog . . . I have to.' He laughs a little, sympa-
thetically. 'Gotta go for the underdog.'*

*It is then that I look at the fight, for the first time.*

*'Hey.'*

*Something is strange.*

'Hey,' I ask the guy again, because there is only one fighter inside the huge, loud, throbbing circle. A boy. He is throwing punches wildly and moving around and blocking and swinging his arms at nothing. 'Hey, how come there's only the one fella fighting?' It is the guy next to me again that I have asked.

He doesn't look at me this time, no. He keeps focused on the boy in the circle, who fights on so intensely that no one can take their eyes off him.

The guy speaks to me.

An answer.

He says, 'He's fighting the world.' And now, I watch as the underdog in the middle of the circle fights on and stands and falls and returns to his haunches and feet and fights on again. He fights on, no matter how hard he hits the ground. He gets up. Some people cheer him. Others laugh now and rubbish him.

Feeling comes out of me.

I watch.

My eyes swell, and burn.

'Can he win?'

I ask it, and now, I too cannot take my eyes off the boy in the circle.

# 9

On the Sunday, Rube copped another hammering on the football paddock, Steve's side lost without him, and I wandered the streets a little bit. I didn't feel like going home that day. Sometimes you just don't. You know. It was time to take stock of things.

At first, I allowed the sullen events of the previous day to cloud my path as I walked. I walked beyond Lumsden Oval, deeper into the city, and I have to tell you that there are so many weirdos in the city that by the time I made it home, I was actually feeling glad I made it back at all.

I was wearing jeans and desert boots and I'd had a shower in the morning and actually washed my hair. As I walked I still felt it sticking up in that un-controllable way, as if it was out to expose me. Still, I felt OK about being clean.

*Maybe the old man's right*, I thought to myself. *All that carryin' on he goes on with about us bein' dirty and a disgrace . . . I guess it feels OK to be clean.*

The usual shops crept back from me as I went past. Milk-bar places. Fish 'n' chips. I also walked past a barbershop and there was a bald guy in there cutting at a guy's locks with a kind of ferocity that scared me. I always see something like that — some kind of molestation of a human being that can only make me trip or lose my footing with grim surprise. Or fidget with discomfort. That day, I remember it made me try to persuade my hair down, but it was up again right away.

All up, the day and the walk weren't the success or rejuvenation I had been looking for.

I kept walking.

Have you ever done that?

Just walk.

Just walk and have no idea where you're going?

It wasn't a good feeling, but not a bad one either I felt caged and free at the same time, like it was only myself that wouldn't allow me to feel either great or miserable. As normal, traffic echoed around me, adding to the sense of not belonging anywhere. Nothing was fixed. Everything was moving. Turning into something. Exactly like me.

Since when did I have something for a girl in my gut?

Since when did I care about my sister and what was happening in her life?

Since when did I bother caring about the contents of Rube's mind?

Since when did I listen to Success Story Steve and care about whether he looked down at me or not?

Since when did I walk aimlessly around? Walking, almost prowling, through the streets?

Then it hit me.

I was alone.

I was alone.

No denying it.

I was certain.

See, I was never a guy who had a whole heap of friends to belong to. Besides Greg Fienni, I never really had friends. I kind of stayed on my own. I hated it, but I was proud of it too. Cameron Wolfe needed no one. He didn't need to be amongst a pack. Not all of us roam like that. No, all he needed was his instincts. All he needed was himself, and he could survive back-yard boxing matches, robbery missions, and any other shame that came down the alley. So why was I feeling so strange now?

Let's be honest.

It had to be the girl.

It had to.

No.

It was everything.

This was my life.

Getting complicated.

My life, and as I walked along the hurrying street, I saw sky above me. I saw buildings, crummy flats, a grimy cigar shop, another barber, electric wires, rubbish in gutters. A derelict asked me for cash but I had none. There was city all around me, breathing in and out like the lungs of a smoker.

Almost instantly, I stopped walking when I knew that all the good feeling had vanished from me. Maybe it slipped out of me and was given to the derelict. Maybe it disappeared somewhere in my stomach and I didn't even notice. All there was now was this anxiety I couldn't explain. What a sight What a feeling. This was terrible: a skinny kid standing, alone. That was the bottom line. Alone, and I didn't feel equipped to handle it. Very suddenly. Yes, quite suddenly, I didn't feel like I could handle my feeling of aloneness.

Was this how it was always going to be?

Would I always live with this kind of self-doubt, and doubt for the civilization around me? Would I always feel so small that it hurt and that even the greatest outcry roaring from my throat was, in reality, just a whimper? Would my footsteps always stop so suddenly and sink into the footpath?

Would I always?

Would I?

Would?

This was terrible, but I dug my feet from out of the footpath and continued walking.

*Don't think*, I told myself. *Think nothingness*. But even nothingness was something. It was a thought. It was a thought, and gutters were still full of the loosened stuffed guts of the city.

I didn't feel like I could cope with this, but I walked on regardless, trying to dig up a new idea that would make things better again.

*Can't worry yourself like this*, I advised myself a bit later, when I reached Central Station. I hung around in the newsagent's for a while, looking at *Rolling Stone* and all that kind of thing. It was a waste of time, of course, but I did it anyway. If I'd had the money on me I would have got a train to the quay, just to set my eyes on the bridge and the water and the boats there. Maybe there would be a mime there or some other poor sap I couldn't give money to anyway because I had none on me. But then, if I had the money for the train, maybe I would have it too for a humble busker. Maybe I could even have taken a ferry ride over the harbour. Maybe. Maybe . . .

The word *maybe* was beginning to annoy me, because the only thing that was fixed was that *maybe* would be with me for ever.

Maybe the girl had something inside her for me.

Maybe Sarah and Bruce would be OK.

Maybe Steve would get back to work and on the paddock as quickly as he wanted. Maybe one day he wouldn't look down at me.

Maybe my old man would be proud of me one day, maybe when we finished off the Conlon job.

Maybe my mother wouldn't have to stand over the stove at night, cooking mushrooms and sausages after working all day.

Maybe *I* could cook.

Maybe Rube would tell me what was going on in his head one night. Or maybe he would grow a beard down to his feet and become some kind of wise man.

Maybe I would end up with a couple of good mates at some point.

Maybe this would all go away tomorrow.

Maybe not.

*Maybe I oughta just walk down to Circular Quay,* I thought, but decided against it, because one thing that wasn't a maybe was that Mum and Dad would fold me if I came in late.

After fifty times of hearing that guy over the loud-speaker saying, 'The train on Platform Seventeen goes to MacArthur' or wherever it was going, I walked home, seeing all my doubt from the other side. Have you ever seen that? Like when you go on holiday. On the way back, everything is the same but it looks a little different than it did on the way. It's because you're seeing it backwards.

That's how it felt, and when I made it home, I shut our half-broken, half-hearted small front gate and went in and sat on the couch. Next to that stinking pillow. Across from Steve.

After half an hour of a *Get Smart* repeat and part of the news, Rube entered the room. He sat down, looked at his watch, and said, 'Bloody hell, Mum sure is draggin' the chain with dinner.'

I looked at him.

Maybe I knew him.

Maybe I didn't.

I knew Steve because he was less complicated.

Winners always are. They know exactly what they want and how they're going to get it.

'Just as long as it isn't the usual,' I talked over to Rube.

'The what?'

'The usual dinner.'

'Oh yeah.' He paused. 'That's all she cooks, though, isn't it?'

I have to admit right now that all the dinner complaining really shames me now, especially with the way people on the city streets are begging for food. The fact is, the complaining happened.

Still, though, I was over the moon when I found out we weren't having mushrooms that Sunday night.

Maybe things were finally looking up.

Then again, maybe not.


*I'm running.*

*Chasing something that doesn't seem to exist, and time and time again I tell myself that I'm chasing nothing. I tell myself to stop, but I never do.*

*The city is thrashed around me by broad daylight, but there is no one on the streets. There is no one in the buildings, flats, or houses. There is no one in anything. The trains and buses drive themselves. They know what to do. They breathe* out but never seem to breathe in. It's just a steady outpour of non-emotion, and I am alone.

Coca-Cola is spilled down the road. It flows into the drains like blood.

Car horns blow.

Brakes snort and then the cars carry on.

I walk.

No people.

No people.

It's weird, I think, how everything can just carry on without all the people. Maybe it's that the people are there but I just can't see them. Their lives have worn them away from my vision. Perhaps their empty souls have swallowed them.

Voices.

Do I hear voices?

At an intersection, a car pulls up and I feel someone staring at me — but it is emptiness that stares at me. When the car leaves, I hear a voice, but it fades.

I run.

I chase the car, ignoring blaring don't-walk signals that flash their red legs at me and beat at my ears, just in case I'm blind.

Am I blind?

No. I see.

I keep running and the entire city swipes past me like

I'm driven by some human-alien force. I bump into invisible people and keep running. I see . . . cars, road, pole, bus, white line, yellow line, crossing, Walk, stutter, Don't Walk, smog, gutter, don't trip, milk bar, gun shop, cheap knives, reggae, disco, live girls, Calvin Klein billboard with woman and man in underwear — enormous. Wires, monorail, green light, orange, red, all three, go, stop, run, run, cross, Turn left anytime with care, Howard Showers, drain, Save East Timor, wall, window, spirit, Gone for lunch, back in five minutes.

No time.

I run, till my trousers are torn and my shoes are simply the bottoms of my feet with some material around the ankles. My toes bleed. I splash through Coke and beer. It dribbles up my legs, then down.

No one is there.

Where is everyone?

Where?

No faces, just movement.

I fall. I'm out. Cracked head on gutter. Awaken.

Later.

Things have changed, and now, people are everywhere. They're everywhere they should be, in the buses, trains, on the street.

'Hey,' I say to the man in the suit waiting for the walk

sign to clock on. He acts like he may have heard something, but walks on when the right sign arrives.

People come right at me, and I swear they are trying to trample me.

Then I realize.

They come right at me because they can't see me.

Now it's me who is invisible.

# 10

During the week, I must confess, Rube and I were up to old tricks. Again. We couldn't help ourselves.

Robberies were out.

One Punch. Out.

So what the hell else was there for us to do?

The decision I came to was back-yard soccer, or football, or whatever you please to call it.

For starters, we had to. We did.

I promise.

Maybe I asked Rube if he wanted to get into it because he was still so miserable about the whole street-sign debacle. Admittedly, it was demoralizing, to actually succeed and then find a way to make yourself fail again. It hurt more than Rube could relate. He just sat there every afternoon and rubbed his gruff jawline with an ominous, melancholic hand. His hair was dirty as ever, strewn over his ears and biting at his back.

'C'mon.' I tried to get him in.

'Nuh.'

It was often like this. Me, being the younger brother, I had always wanted Rube to do things, whether it was a game of Monopoly or a ball game in the back yard. Rube, the older brother, well he was the judge and jury. If he didn't feel like doing it, we didn't do it. Maybe that's why I was always so willing to go on his robbery missions – simply because he actually wanted me to come along. We'd given up on doing things with Steve years ago.

'C'mon,' I kept trying. 'I've got the ball pumped up, and the goals are ready. Come have a look. They're chalked onto the fence at both ends.'

'The same size?'

'Two metres wide, nearly one and a half high.'

'Good, good.'

He looked up and gave a slight smile, for the first time in days.

'We on?' I asked again, with far too much eagerness.

'OK.'

We went outside then and it was lovely.

Absolutely lovely.

Rube fell to the cement and got up. Twice. He

swore his head off at me when I scored, and it was getting serious. An out-of-control shot at goal went flying to the top of the fence, we held our breath, then let it out when it hit the edge and came back. We even smiled at each other.

It was brilliant mainly because Rube had been down and out with his own form of identity crisis while I was in my typical agony over the whole Rebecca Conlon affair. This was much better. Yes. It was, because all of a sudden we were back to doing the things we did best — throwing ourselves and each other around the back-yard and getting dirty and making sure to swear and carry on and, if possible, offend the neighbours. This was better all right. This was a welcome return to the good old days.

The ball thumped into the fence, making next-door's dog bark and the caged parrots over there go wild. I copped a whack in the shins. Rube fell on the concrete again, taking some skin off his hand when he braced himself for the landing. All the while that dog next door kept barking and those parrots were in some kind of frenzy. It was old times all right, and typically, Rube won, 7–6. I didn't care, though, because both of us ended up laughing and not taking things so seriously.

What greeted us on the back step was, however, something very different.

It was Sarah, alone.

First to notice her was Rube. He back-handed me lightly on the arm and motioned over to her with his head.

I looked.

I said very quietly, 'Oh, no.'

Sarah looked up then because she must have heard me, and I promise you, the way she looked was bad. She was sitting there, all crumpled up, with her knees up to her shoulders and her arms folded, holding them up as if to keep all air inside her. Tears cut down her face.

Awkward.

That's exactly how it was when we walked over to our sister and stood on each side of her, looking at her and feeling things and not knowing what to do.

Eventually, I sat down next to her but I had no idea what to say.

In the end, it was Sarah who broke the silence. The dog next door had settled down, and the neighbourhood seemed stunned by this event occurring in our back yard. It was like it could sense it. It could sense some form of tragedy and helplessness being played out, and to tell you the truth, it all surprised me. I was so used to things just going on, oblivious and ignorant to all feeling.

Sarah spoke.

She spoke. 'He got someone else.'

'Bruce?' I asked, to which Rube looked down at me with an incredulous face on him.

'No,' he barked, 'the king of bloody Sweden. Who do y' think?'

'OK, all right!'

Then Sarah leaned away and said, 'I think you'd better leave me alone for a while.'

'OK.'

As I stood up and left with Rube, the city around us seemed colder than ever again, and I realized that even if it really had sensed something going on, it certainly didn't care. It moved forward again. I could feel it. I could almost hear it laugh and taste it. Close. Watching. Mocking. And it was cold, so cold, as it watched my sister bleeding at the back of our house.

Inside, Rube was angry.

He said, 'Now, you see? This spoils things.'

'It was always gonna happen.' As I said it, I saw Steve's figure out on the front porch. Away from us.

'Yeah, but why today?'

'Why not?'

From the couch, I looked at an old photo of Steve, Sarah, Rube and me as very young children, standing in staggered formation for some photographer man. Steve smiled. Sarah smiled. We all did. It was strange to see it, because it was there every day and only now was I really noticing it. Steve's smile. It cared — for us. Sarah's smile. It was beautiful. Rube and I looked clean. All four of us were young and undaunted and our smiles were so strong that it made me smile even then on the couch, with a kind of loss.

*Where did that go?* I asked inside me. I couldn't even remember the photo being taken. Was it actually real?

At that moment, Sarah was on our back step, crying, and Rube and I were slumped on the couch, powerless to help her. Steve didn't seem to care, for any of us.

*Where did it go?* I thought again. How could that picture turn into this one?

Had years defeated us?

Had they worn us down?

Had they passed like big white clouds, disintegrating very slowly so that we couldn't notice?

In any case, this was pretty awful, and it was to worsen.

It worsened during the night when Sarah went out and didn't come back for hours.

She left with the words 'I'm goin' out for a walk,' and a lot of time passed while she was gone. The rest of us acted indifferent to it at first, but by just after eleven, we were all worried. Even Steve seemed a bit affected.

'C'mon,' our father told us. 'We're goin' out lookin'.'

No one argued.

Rube and I went out in the panel van with Dad while Mum and Steve stayed home in case Sarah showed up while we were gone. We checked the pubs and all her friends' places. Even Bruce's place. Empty. She was nowhere.

By midnight, when we got home, she still wasn't back, and all we could do now was wait.

We each did it differently.

Mum sat, silent, not looking at anyone.

Dad made coffee after coffee and drank them down like there was no tomorrow.

Steve put a heat pack on and off his ankle and kept it elevated, determined.

Rube mumbled something very quietly, at least five hundred times: 'I'm gonna kill that bastard. I'm gonna kill that bastard. I'm gonna get that Bruce Patterson. I'm gonna kill that . . . I'm gonna. I'm gonna . . .'

As for me, I ground my teeth together a bit and leaned forward with my chin resting on the table.

Only Rube went to bed.

The rest of us stayed.

'No sign?' Mum asked when she woke up at one o'clock.

'No.' Dad shook his head, and quite soon, we were all falling asleep, under a white, aching kitchen light globe.

Later on, a dream was arriving.

Interruption.

'Cam?'

'Cam?'

I was shaken awake.

I jumped.

'Sarah?'

'Nah, me.'

It was Rube.

'Ah, bloody you!'

'Yeah.' He grinned. 'She's still not here?'

108

'No. Unless she walked straight past us to bed.'

'Nah, she's not in there.'

That was when we noticed something else – now Steve was gone as well.

I checked the basement.

'Nup.' I looked back up at Rube. So now just the two of us went out on the porch, then out on the street. Where the hell was he?

'Wait.' Rube turned round, looking down the road. 'There he is.'

We saw our brother sitting, propped up against a telegraph pole. We ran down to him. We stopped. Rube asked, 'What's goin' on?'

Steve looked up, and I had never seen him afraid like that, or as knotted up. He looked so lanky, and still like a man; he had always seemed to be a man. Always . . . but never like this. Not a vulnerable one.

His crutches were two dead arms, lying there, wooden, next to him.

Slowly, meltingly, our brother said, 'I guess.' He stopped. Started again. 'I just wanted to find her.'

We said nothing, but I think when we helped Steve up and helped him walk home, he must have seen what the lives of Rube, Sarah and me were like. He'd seen what it was to fall down and not know if you could get back up, and it scared him. It scared him because we did get up. We always did. We always.

We took him home.

We—

From there, we all waited in the kitchen again, but only Rube and I were awake. At one point, he whispered something to me. The same thing as before.

He went, 'Ay, Cam. We're gonna get that Patterson bloke.' He sounded so sure of it. 'We'll get him.'

I was too tired to say anything but 'We will.'

Pretty soon, Rube was asleep, like Mum, Dad and Steve. It didn't take long for my own eyes to feel like cement and I went as well.

All of us, asleep in the kitchen.

I dreamed.

It's coming up.

Not a bad one.

When I woke up again, there was an extra person now, sleeping like the rest of us, at the crowded kitchen table.

*I'm standing in an empty goal. The stadium is packed. Perhaps 120,000 people have their eyes glued to me.*

*They chant.*

*'Wolf Man! Wolf Man!'*

*I look around the entire stadium, at all the people willing me on, and I love them, even though they are complete strangers to me. I think they're South Americans or something. Brazilians or something. Maybe Argentinians.*

*'I won't let you down,' I whisper to them, knowing they couldn't hear me even if I screamed to them.*

*In front of me, there is a line of people, all in the opposition's colours.*

*They are the people from my story:*

*Dad, Rube, Mum, Steve, Sarah, Bruce, Bruce's faceless new girlfriend, Greg, the dental nurse, the dentist, Dennison the principal, Welfare Woman, Rube's mates and Rebecca Conlon.*

*I'm wearing all the stuff the goalkeeper has to wear: boots, socks pulled up, a green jersey with a diamond pattern on the front, and gloves. It's night and the black air is busted through by huge lights standing like watchtowers, over all of us.*

*I'm ready.*

*I slap my hands together and crouch, ready to dive either way for the ball. The goal behind me feels kilometres wide and kilometres deep. The net is a loose cage, swaying and whispering in the breeze.*

*Dad steps up, places the ball, calls out that this is some kind of cup final penalty shootout, and that everything depends on me. He walks back, props, and runs and drills the ball to my right. I dive but the ball is way out of reach. He looks at me after the ball flies into the corner of the net, and he smiles, as if to say, 'Sorry, boy. I had to.'*

*Mum steps up. Then Rube. They both score, Rube with a callous smile. He says, 'You've got no hope, sunshine.'*

*The crowd through all of this is always buzzing, like static in my ear. When I am beaten and the ball scores, they roar and then sigh, because they are on my side. They want me to save one because they know how hard I'm fighting. They see my small arms and the will on my lips, and they cannot hear, but feel the smacking of my hands when I ready myself for each penalty kick. They still chant.*

*My name.*

*My name.*

*Yet, no matter how hard I try, I can't save a single goal.*

*A miserable Sarah even gets through me. Before her shot, she says, 'Don't try to help me. It's pointless. All is out of your control.'*

*Steve goes, and Bruce. Rube's mates. Everyone.*

*Then Rebecca Conlon steps up.*

*She walks towards me.*

*Slowly.*

*Smiling.*

*She says: 'If you save it, I'll love you.'*

*I nod, solemnly, ready.*

*She goes back, comes in, kicks the ball.*

*It's up high and I lose it in the lights. I find it and dive, high to the right, and somehow, when the ball hits my wrist, it comes back and hits me hard in the face.*

*I come down with it.*

*It pops out when I land and it rolls, so slowly, over the line and into the back of the net.*

*Oh, I dive for it, but it's no use. I fall short — and quickly, I'm alone, not in the stadium but in our sun-drenched back yard, sitting against the fence with a bloodied nose.*

# 11

Our plan was to get him quickly. No point letting a week or two pass. If we did, maybe the burning desire to really put it to the guy would fade. There was no way we could afford that.

We found out that this Bruce Patterson had been getting it off with some other girl for about a month, thus leading our sister on by still coming over. It was a slap in the head for all of us that we allowed him into our house when he was into it with some scrubber around the city.

'Should we go bash him?' I asked Rube, but he only looked at me, with ridicule.

'Are you serious? Look at the size of y'. You're like a Chihuahua and Patterson's built like a brick bloody shithouse. Do you have any idea what the guy would do to you?'

'Well, I thought maybe the two of us.'

'I'm a weed myself,' was Rube's curt response to

that one. 'Sure, I've got a hell of a beard goin', but Bruce could kill the pair of us.'

'Yeah, you're right.'

What happened next was unexpected.

There was a knock at the door that was more like scraping, and when I opened it, my former best mate Greg was standing there.

'Can I come in?' he asked me.

'Watta y' reckon?'

I opened the flyscreen door and he entered the house, just after taking a look over at Steve, who sat grim-faced as ever on the porch.

'Hey, werewolf,' Greg greeted Rube inside, to which Rube threatened to throw him out.

'Sorry,' he apologized, and I took him into Rube's and my room.

He sat down under the window, against the wall. Silent.

'Well,' I asked, sitting on my bed, 'if you don't mind my asking, but what the hell brings you here?'

'I need help,' was the swift, frank reply. He rummaged his hands through his hair and I could see the 'druff go flying out. Greg always had a bit of a dandruff problem. He enjoyed it, shaking it out on the desk in school.

'Help with what?' I kept probing.

'Money.'

'How much?'

'Three hundred.'

'*Three hundred!* Bloody hell, what the hell've you been doin' lately?'

'Ah, don't ask. Just . . .' His face flinched a bit. 'You got it?'

'Geez, three hundred, I d'know.'

I went to my piece of carpet and got out what was stashed under there. Eighty bucks.

'Well, I've got eighty here.' I got out my bank-book thing and saw that I had a hundred and thirty in it. 'So I've got two-ten all up. That's the best I can do.'

'Ah, damn, mate.'

I joined him on the floor, against my bed, asking, 'Just tell me what it's for, will y'?'

He was reluctant.

'Tell me or I won't give y' the cash.' This was a lie and we both knew it. We both knew I was giving Greg my money and I wouldn't even ask for it back. That was all there was to it. But he owed me at least this. He owed it to me to say where my money was going.

'Ah,' he gave out. 'One of me mates, Dale. You know 'im?'

Dale Perry.

Yeah, I knew him all right. He was exactly the kind of guy I hated because he walked around like he owned the joint no matter where he went, and I hated his guts. In Commerce the previous year (a subject I should never have chosen), he had taken his metal ruler, heated it up on the heater, and then held it up against my ear, burning the absolute hell out of me. That's who Dale Perry was. He was also in that big group chatting with the pretty girls at the football that day.

'Yeah, I know the guy,' I stated calmly.

'Yeah, well, a few of his older mates, they needed someone to pick some gear up for 'em. Three hundred bucks' worth.'

'Gear?'

Of course, I knew exactly what the gear was, but I thought I'd make this whole thing just a little uncomfortable for Greg. After all, I was giving the guy every cent I had on me. So much for buying myself a stereo or whatever. So much for that hard-earned cash I'd got working the past few weeks with Dad. It was all getting flushed down the toilet because a former best mate of mine came to me because he knew I was the only guy who wouldn't let him down. None of his new mates would help him out, but his original one would.

It's weird.

Don't you think?

It's not so much that the old friend is a better friend.

It's just that you know the person better, and you know they don't really care if you're acting like a poor, grovelling idiot. They know you would do the same for them. I knew Greg would do it for me if it was the other way around.

So yes, 'Gear?' I asked him. 'What are y' talkin' about?'

'You know,' he answered.

I let him get away with it. 'Yeah, I know,'

'Just light stuff,' he went on, 'but a whole lot of it. There were about ten guys and they all threw in and they were all too lazy to go get it 'emselves.' He slipped down against the wall a little further. 'I got the stuff no problems, but things got bad when I had to sit on it for a night.'

'Aah.' I threw my head back and started laughing.

I was pretty sure I knew now exactly what had happened.

'Yeah, that's right.' Greg nodded. 'Me old bloody lady found it under my bed and the old man threw it in the fire. It was like signing my death warrant . . . I can't believe the old boy chucked it in the fire, ay.'

By now, I was in stitches, because I could just see Greg's old man – a tiny, curly-haired, wiry brute of a man swearing his head off and throwing it into the fire. It actually got Greg laughing as well, even though he kept saying, 'It's not funny, Cam. It's not funny.'

It was, though, and that was what saved him for the money.

It saved him because I told the story to Rube and he shelled out the extra ninety bucks Greg needed, even though he threatened to kill him if he didn't get it back in a fair hurry. The solution ended up being that I would pay Rube back from the money I earned with Dad over the next month or so and everyone was happy. Then Greg would pay the lot back to me.

For Greg, you could see the pressure released from his face. He didn't look so drawn once that cash had found its way into his hand.

In the next room, Sarah was lying on her bed in a hundred pieces.

We walked past her on our way out back, where Rube, Greg and I took potshots at goal against the fence. We took turns at being goalie. It was my idea (mainly because of the dream I'd had the night before), and I was actually just hoping I wouldn't get a bleeding nose. Although, Rebecca Conlon wasn't in the yard, was she? I thought I was pretty safe.

Of course, next-door's dog started barking and the parrots went berserk.

It was all heightened when Rube phoned his mates. This was the conversation:

'Hello.'

'Hello, Simon. Ruben here,'

'Ruben. How are you?'

'I'm well. Y' comin' over?'

'Why not indeed. That sounds convenient enough.'

'Get Cheese an' Jeff.'

'Right.'

'Goodbye.'

'Goodbye.'

When they made it to our place, we got a fully fledged game going.

Over and over, we hammered the ball into the fence, making the most of the time we had before Mum and Dad got home. You should have heard it. *Smash. Smash.* The ball at both ends was killing it and the sound echoed around everywhere, followed by the shrieks and the swearing.

My team was Jeff, Greg and myself and we were actually winning, even though we were smaller and weaker than Rube's team. It was our hunger.

Four—two it was when next-door's dog stopped barking.

'Stop, stop!' I shouted when I noticed. 'You hear that?'

'What?'

'The dog.'

'Hey, yeah. It's stopped barkin'.'

I climbed up the fence and peeked over, and you won't believe what I saw.

The dog was dead.

'Geez, I think it's dead,' I said, looking back at everyone else.

'What!?'

'I'm tellin' y's. Come have a look.'

Rube climbed up next to me and could only agree.

'Bloody 'ell, I think he's right,' he laughed back

down to the others. 'I think we've given the poor bloody thing a heart attack.'

'Y'sure?'

'Or a stroke.'

'Oh no,' I said. 'What have we done?'

'What sort of dog is it?'

Rube had had enough.

'I don't bloody know!' he yelled down at Cheese. 'I think it's a, a—'

'Pomeranian,' I answered for him.

'What the hell's a Pomeranian?'

'You know,' Cheese explained to the others, 'one of those fluffy rodent-lookin' things . . . I guess he just barked till he couldn't take it any more.'

Even the parrots over in the cage were looking morosely down at the dog.

'We've gotta do somethin',' I said to Rube.

'Like what? Give it mouth to mouth?'

'Look, it's shakin'.'

'Oh, this is lovely, ay.'

I jumped over and took off my flanno shirt and wrapped up the dog. Rube came over and the rest of the fellas looked over the fence as we stroked the fluffy rodent-looking dog, wondering if it really was about to die.

After about fifteen minutes, our next-door neighbour came home — a fifty-year-old fella with a mouth fouler than all of us put together. He showed a lot of restraint, to tell you the truth, as he raced out back, called us a few names, picked up the Pomeranian — whose name was Miffy by the way — and took it to the vet.

'Y' think it'll live?' we asked each other, back at our place.

'Mate, I d'know.'

Gradually, everyone left. Greg was last.

'Man.' He shook his head on his way out. 'I'd fogotten what it's like round here.'

'Old times, ay?'

'Yeah,' he nodded. 'Chaos.'

'Absolutely.'

It really had been like old times, but I knew it was fruitless to think it would go on. We both knew that the next time he came over would be to pay either some or all of my money back. It was just the way things were.

In the evening, something I knew was coming came. The neighbour.

He came over telling Mum and Dad that they couldn't control Rube and me, and because Rube was the only one out of us with any money left, he was the one who paid the man's vet bill.

Miffy the Pomeranian, by the way, was OK. It was just a very mild heart attack. Poor rodent midget dog.

It was all pretty much the last straw for our mother, though.

She had us sitting at the kitchen table and she circled us, shouting and telling us off like you wouldn't believe. She even held the wooden spoon under our noses, even though she hadn't hit us with it since I was ten. I tell you, she looked ready to wrap it around our heads.

'Why do you keep doing this!?' she screamed at us. 'Giving each other black eyes, giving bloody neighbours' dogs heart attacks. It's a disgrace . . . I'm ashamed of you both. *Again!*'

Even Dad could only sit in the corner, completely silent. He didn't dare to speak himself for fear of being the next to be set upon.

At the end, she really went crazy, getting the compost off the kitchen sink, and instead of taking it outside to put it in her compost bin, she threw it to the floor, picked it up, and threw it down again, this time at my feet.

'You're like animals!' she shouted with even more

volume than earlier. Then she said the thing that always seems to hurt the most: '*Grow up!*'

Needless to say, Rube and I cleaned up the mess and took it outside and stayed out there. We didn't dare to go back in.

From her bedroom window, Sarah looked out at us and smiled, shaking her head through her suffering. She was laughing, which made us laugh a bit ourselves. It made Rube find his resolve again and say, 'We're still gettin' Patterson. Make no mistake about that.'

'We've gotta,' I agreed.

After a longer while, I reflected on the day's proceedings, because now I owed Rube half the vet's bill as well. Things had really gone downhill, I promise you.

'Damn that Pomeranian,' I suggested.

'Huh,' Rube snorted. 'Pomeranian with a weak heart. It could only happen to us, ay.'

*There's a guy in front of me on a dirt road at sunrise.*

*He looks at me.*

*I look at him.*

*We stand, maybe ten metres apart, until finally I decide to break the silence.*

I say, 'So?'

'So what?' comes his reply. He's wearing a robe and scratches his beard and tries to get a stone out of one of his sandals.

'Well, I don't know,' I think to say. 'Who the hell are you, for starters?'

He smiles.

Laughs.

Stands.

When he's ready, he repeats the question and answers it: 'Who the hell am I?' A brief laugh. 'I'm Christ.'

'Christ? You actually exist?'

'Of course I bloody do.'

I decide to test Him.

'So who am I, then?'

'I'm not interested in who you are,' and He walks towards me along the road, still trying to get that pebble out of His sandal. 'Bloody sandals.' He scuffs, then continues. 'Actually, I'm interested in what you are.'

'Which is?'

'Miserable.'

'Yeah.' I shrug in agreement.

'I can help,' He goes on, and I'm expecting Him now to give me the usual line all those scripture teachers give us on their annual pilgrimage to our school. He doesn't.

Instead, He hands me a bottle with red liquid in it and motions with hands saying, 'Bottoms up,' for me to drink it.

'What is it?' I ask.

'Wine.'

'Yeah?'

'Actually, no, it's red cordial — you're too young to be drinking.'

'Aah, y' wet blanket.'

'Hey, don't blame me. It's not my fault, I'm telling you. It was me old man who wouldn't let me give you the real thing. So you can blame Him.'

'OK, OK . . . What's up with Him anyway?'

'Ah, He's been under a lot of pressure lately.'

'The Middle East?'

'Yeah, they're at it again.' He comes closer and whispers, 'Just between you and me, He was close to calling the whole thing off last week.'

'What? The world?'

'Yep.'

'Christ almighty!'

Christ's face looks disappointed at my words.

'Oh, yeah. Sorry,' I say. 'That sort of talk's no good, ay.'

'No worries. Look.' Jesus has decided it's time to get down to business. 'I really came to give you this.'

He pulls something out of a robe pocket and I ask, 'What's that?'

'Oh, it's just some ointment.' He hands it to me. 'For the bleeding nose.'

'Oh, great. Thanks very much.'

# 12

If you're wondering if we ever did get our mate Bruce Patterson, well, we didn't. We planned it out and everything, but we just never went through with it. There were more important issues at hand at home, like the frostiness that was afforded to Rube and me by Mum and Dad. They were obviously pretty unhappy about the kind of lives we were leading, and the way we had this knack of embarrassing them. You might also think that this frostiness may have dampened our enthusiasm for somehow getting back at Bruce for Sarah, but it didn't. Not really. Steve told us to let it go as well. He was back to his 'I'm better than you people' routine and he told us we were idiots. It all intimidated me just a little, but not Rube. He was as keen as ever, and he truly believed that we weren't responsible for next-door's dog having a heart attack. He explained to me that we couldn't help it if the stupid mutt was weak as water.

'Hell, it's not illegal to play soccer in your own back yard, is it?' he asked me.

'I guess not.'

'You know not.'

'I s'pose.

Stewing over it for a few days, Rube finally came into our room and told me what the plan was and what it all meant. He said, 'Cam, this is gonna be my last job.' You'd think the guy was Al Capone or something. 'See, after this last effort, I'm retiring from the robbery, thieving, vandalism game.'

'How can you retire if you never even had a career?'

'Ah, shut up, will y'. I admit I've had my ups and downs, but it's gotta stop right here. I can't believe I'm sayin' this, but I've gotta grow up.'

I thought for a while, in disbelief, then asked, 'So what are we doin'?'

'Simple,' was the answer. 'Eggs.'

'Ah, come on.' I turned away. 'We can do a lot better than lousy eggs.'

'No, we can't,' and this was the first time I'd heard Rube speak on this subject with reality in his voice. 'The truth, mate, is that we're hopeless.'

To this I could only nod. I then said, 'All right,'

and it was decided that we would go to Bruce Patterson's house on Friday night and egg that beautiful red car of his. Maybe his front door and windows too. I was truly glad as well that this was the last time because I was getting sick of it.

Another unavoidable fact also made this whole thing harder than it should have been. It was the fact that I still couldn't get my mind off Rebecca Conlon. I just couldn't, no matter how hard I tried. I thought of her and wondered if she would be there this week, or if she would be off again, having a life without me. It hurt sometimes, while at others I convinced myself that it was all far too risky. *Just look at Bruce and Sarah*, I told myself. *I bet that guy was as obsessed with Sarah as I am with this other girl, and I bet he promised himself never to hurt her, just like I've been doin' – and look what he's done to her. He's left her a crumpled mess, lyin' on her bed all the time.*

When Friday evening came, I think Rube and I were too tired to go through with it. We were sick of ourselves, and with two cartons of eggs sitting in our room, we decided not to go.

'Ah, well, that's it, then.' Rube said it. 'If you have to think about it so long, it isn't worth doin'.'

'Well, what are we gonna do with all these eggs?' I asked.

'Eat 'em, I s'pose.'

'What? Twelve each?'

'I guess.'

For the time being, we left the eggs under Rube's bed, but I myself still took a trip out to Bruce's place.

I went down there after dinner and walked past his car and imagined myself throwing eggs at it. The thought was ridiculous, to say the least.

It made me laugh as I knocked on the door, though the smile was wiped off my face when a girl I assumed was Sarah's replacement answered. She opened up and stared at me through the flyscreen.

'Bruce around?' I asked her.

She nodded. 'You wanna come in?'

'Nah, I'll be right.' I waited out on the porch.

When Bruce saw me, he looked pretty confused. It wasn't like he and I had been good mates or anything. It wasn't like we had a pool and he'd thrown me around in it or as if we'd kicked footballs around together. No, we'd barely even talked, and I could see he was afraid that I might be here to give him a serve. I wasn't.

All I did was wait for him to come out of the house so we could talk. Just one question. That was all I had, as we leaned on his front railing, looking onto the street.

I asked it.

'When you first met my sister . . . did you promise yourself never to hurt her?'

There was silence for a while, but then he answered.

He said, 'Yeah, I did,' and after a few more seconds, I left.

He called out, 'Hey, Cameron.'

I turned round.

'How is she?'

I smiled, raising my head, resolute. 'She's OK. She's good.'

He nodded and I told him, 'See y' later.'

'Yeah, see y' later, mate.'

At home, the night wasn't finished. An act not of vandalism but of symbolism was to occur.

At around eight-thirty, Rube walked into our room and something was different. What was it?

His beard was gone.

When he presented his post-animal face to the rest of the family, there were claps and sighs of relief. No more animalistic face. No more animalistic behaviour.

I myself kept hearing Bruce Patterson telling me that he had promised to never hurt my sister. It hunted me, even as I sat through an extremely violent movie on TV. I kept hearing his voice, and I wondered if I would ever hurt Rebecca Conlon if she would let me get near her in the first place. I was hunted all night.

*It's jungle and I'm with her. I can't see her face, but I know I'm with Rebecca Conlon. I lead her by the hand and we are moving very fast, ducking around twisted trees whose fingers are branches spread like cracked ceiling under grey sky.*

*'Faster,' I tell her.*

*'Why?' is her reply.*

*'Because he's coming.'*

*'Who's coming?'*

*I don't answer her because I don't know. The only thing I am completely sure of is that I can hear footsteps behind us through the jungle. I can hear a hunching forward, coming after us.*

*'Come on,' I say to her again.*

*We come to a river and plunge in, wading hurriedly across the freezing cold water.*

*On the other side, I see something upriver and I lead her there. It's a cave that crouches down amongst some heavy trees above the water.*

*We go in. No words. No 'In here.'*

*She smiles, relieved.*

*I don't see it.*

*I know it.*

*We sit down right in the back corner of the cave, and we hear the meditative water of the river outside, climbing down, down. Slow. Real. Knowing.*

*She falls.*

*Asleep.*

*'It's OK,' I tell her, and I feel her in my arms. My own eyes try to sleep as well, but they don't. They stay wide awake as time snarls forward and silence drops down, like measured thought. I can't even hear the river any more.*

*When.*

*The figure enters the cave.*

*He walks in and pauses.*

*He sees.*

*Us.*

*He has a weapon.*

*He looks.*

*Smiles.*

*Even though I can't see his face, I know he smiles.*

'What do you want?' I ask, afraid but quiet so I won't wake the girl in my arms.

The figure says nothing. He keeps stepping forward. Slow. Reeling. No.

There's a sound, like, a slit, and smoke rises from the weapon the figure is holding. It rises up to his face and wraps itself around it. It tells me that something terrible has happened, and Rebecca Conlon stirs slightly on my lap.

A match is struck.

Light.

I look at her.

Know!

This.

She's hurt, for sure, because I see blood dripping from her heart. Slow. Real.

I look up. The figure holds the lit match and I see his face. His eyes and lips and expression belong to me.

'But you promised,' I tell him, and I scream, to try and wake up. I need to wake up and know that I would never ever hurt her.

# 13

As usual, Dad and I went to work on Saturday, at the Conlon place.

Rather than keep you in suspense (if you even still care by now), I might as well let you know that this time she was there, and she was as brilliant as ever.

I was still working under the house when she came to me.

'Hey, I missed you last week,' I said when she showed, and immediately chastised myself in my head – the statement was so ambiguous. I mean, did it mean *I missed you* as in I just didn't see you (which was the intended message), or did it mean *I was really heartbroken that you weren't here, y' stupid bitch?* I wasn't sure what messages I was sending out. Overall, I could only hope she thought I was saying we just didn't see each other. You can't seem too desperate in a situation like that, even if your heart is annihilating you from the inside.

She said, 'Well . . .' God, she said it with that

voice that made her real. 'I wasn't here on purpose.'

What the hell was this?

'What?' I dared to ask.

'You heard.' She grinned. 'I wasn't here . . .'

'Because of me?'

She nodded.

Was this bad or good?

It sounded bad. Very bad.

But then, it also sounded good, in some sick, twisted way. Was she having me on?

No.

'I didn't wanna be here because I was' — she swallowed — 'scared to make a fool out of myself like last time.'

'Last time?' I asked, confused. 'Wasn't it me who said something stupid?' It was me all right, who said, 'I like workin' here.' I remembered it and cringed.

We were both crouched down under the house and these wooden beams hovered over us, warning us that one loss of concentration would leave our heads nice and bruised. I made sure not to stand up straight.

'At least you said *something*.' She pushed her argument.

Suddenly, something poured out of me.

I said, 'I wouldn't hurt you. Well, at least I'd try like hell not to. I promise.'

'Pardon?' She stepped away a bit. 'What do you mean?'

'I mean, if . . . Did you have an OK weekend last week?' Drivel. Drivel talk.

'Yeah.' She nodded and stayed where she was. 'I was at a friend of mine's house.' Then she slipped it in. 'And then we went over to this guy's place – Dale.'

Dale.

Why was that name so familiar?

Oh no.

Oh, great.

'Dale Perry?'

Dale Perry,

Greg's mate.

Typical.

A hero like that.

I could tell she really liked the guy.

More than me.

He was a winner.

People liked him.

Greg did.

Though he could depend on me.

'Yeah, Dale Perry,' she replied – confirming my worst fears – nodding and smiling. 'You know him, do you?'

'Yeah, I know him.' It dawned on me then as well that this Rebecca Conlon was most likely one of the girls in the group at Lumsden Oval, on that day that seemed decades ago now. There were a few girls like her there, I remembered. Same real hair. Same real legs. Same . . . It all made sense. She was local, and pretty, and real.

Dale Perry.

I almost mentioned that he'd nearly burned my ear off just over a year ago but held it back. I didn't want her thinking that I was one of those completely jealous guys who hated everyone who was better than himself which actually was exactly the kind of guy I was.

'My best friend reckons he likes me, but I don't know . . .'

She went on talking but I couldn't bring myself to listen. I just couldn't. Why in the hell was she telling me this anyway? Was it because I was just the plumber's son and I went to an old state school while she most likely went to a Saint something-or-other school? 'Was it because I was the kind of guy who was harmless and couldn't bite?

Well, I came close.

I almost stopped her to say, 'Ah, just go away with your Dale Perry,' but I didn't. I loved her too much and I wouldn't hurt her, no matter how much I myself was hurting.

Instead, I asked if she knew Greg.

'Greg Fiennes or something?'

'Fienni.'

'Yeah, I do. How do you know him?'

And for some reason, all these tears started welling up in my eyes.

'Ah,' I said. 'He was a friend of mine once,' and I turned away, to keep working and to hide my eyes.

'A good friend?'

Damn this girl!

'My best friend,' I admitted.

'Oh.' She looked through my back. I could feel it.

I wondered if she was getting the picture here. Maybe. Probably. Yes, probably, because she left then with a far too friendly 'OK, bye-ee.' Had I heard that before? Of course I had, and it gashed my throat with reality.

The whole altercation didn't drive me through the day like the disappointment of last week had. No, this time I limped through it.

I felt something awful in me.

Limping on.

Dad saw me and gave me a serve for being so slow, but I couldn't pick it up. I tried like you wouldn't believe, but my back was broken. My spirit was crushed.

I had the chance to tell her off.

I could have hurt her.

I didn't.

It was no consolation.

As I worked, I constantly had to pull myself together and it was such a struggle. It was like every step was out to get me. Blisters on my hands started opening up and feeling kept creeping into my eyes. I started sniffing at the air to get enough in my lungs, and when the day was over I struggled out from under the house and stood there, waiting. I really wanted to collapse to the ground, but I held it together.

I felt itchy, dirty, diseased – by simply being me. What was wrong with me?

I felt like the dog that's got rabies in this book I was reading in school, *To Kill a Mockingbird*. The dog, it's limping and slobbering all over the road and the father, Atticus, he surprises his son by shooting it.

*   *   *

I'm walking along top a fence line that seems to stretch for an eternity. Somehow, though, I know that it will stop at some point. I know it will last as long as my life.

'Keep walking,' I tell myself.

My arms are out to keep me balanced.

On either side of me, there is air and ground, trying to get me to jump down into it.

Which side do I jump?

It is early, early morning. It's that time when it's still dark but you know the day is coming. Blue is bleeding through black. Stars are dying.

The fence.

Sometimes it's stone, sometimes it's wood, and sometimes it's barbed wire.

I walk it, and still, I am tempted by each side that flanks it.

'Jump,' I hear each side whisper. 'Jump down here.'

Distance.

Out there, somewhere, I can hear dogs barking, although their voices seem human. They bark and when I look all around me I can't see them. I can only hear barking that forms an audience for my journey along this fence.

Purple in the sky.

Pins-and-needles legs.

*Shivers down my right side.*

*Concussion thoughts.*

*Footsteps.*

*Alone.*

*Take one after the other.*

*Barbed wire now.*

*Where do I jump?*

*Who do I listen to?*

*Daisy sun, maroon sky.*

*First part of the sun — a frown.*

*Last part of the sun — a smile.*

*Dark day.*

*Thoughts cover the sky.*

*Thoughts are the sky.*

*Feet on fence.*

*One side of the fence is victory . . .*

*The . . . other side is defeat.*

*Walk.*

*I walk, on.*

*Deciding.*

*Sweat reigns.*

*It lands on me, controlled, and drips down my face.*

*Victory one side.*

*Defeat on the other.*

*Clouds are uncertain.*

*They throb in the sky like drumbeats, like pulses.*

*I decide —*

*Jump.*

*High. High.*

*The wind gets me, and high up, I know that it will throw me down to the side of the fence it wants.*

*Wherever I land, soon enough, I know I will have to climb back up and keep walking, but for now, I'm still in the air.*

# 14

Where did I go from there?

What did I do?

How did things turn out?

Well, this is basically the end, so the answers should be in these next few pages. I doubt they will surprise you, but you never know. I don't know how smart or thick you are. You could be Albert Einstein for all I know, or some literary prizewinner, or maybe you're just middle of the road like me.

So we might as well cut to the chase – I will tell you now how things pretty much finished up in this wintry part of my life. The end began like this:

Moping.

I did it for the whole of Sunday, and on Monday at school. Something churned in me, starting in my stomach and rising till it was reaching its arms up to strip my skin from the inside. It burned.

On Wednesday at school, I had a bit of a

conversation with Greg, mainly because of the beaten-up look of his face.

'What happened to you?' I asked him when I ran into him in one of the walkways.

'Ah, forget it,' he answered me. 'Nothin'.' But we both knew it was really pretty obvious that the fellas he'd bought the gear for were still unimpressed by his efforts, even after he'd come through with the money.

'They got you anyway, ay?' I asked. I smiled mournfully as I said it and Greg smiled as well.

'Yep, they got me,' he nodded. His smile was a knowing, ironic one. 'They decided on giving me a hidin' for the inconvenience I'd caused them . . . The original guy was out of gear so they had to go somewhere else. They weren't impressed.'

'Fair enough,' was my conclusion.

'I s'pose, yeah.'

We parted ways a few moments later, and looking back at him, I looked at Greg and tried praying for him, like all those prayers I had made earlier on in this story, but I couldn't. I just couldn't. Don't ask me why. I hoped that he was OK, but I couldn't summon the strength to pray for it.

What good had my prayers done anyway?

They sure as hell hadn't helped my own cause too much — but remember? I never did get around to praying for myself, did I? Maybe that's what was behind it, though. Myself. Maybe the only reason I'd prayed for others to begin with was to bring myself good fortune. Was that true? Was it? No. No way. It wasn't.

Maybe the prayers did actually work.

It's quite probable when you think about it, because back home, Sarah had started talking on the phone to replace the intense getting-off sessions on the couch, Steve was starting to walk again, Rube had sorted himself out a bit, Mum and Dad seemed happy enough, and no doubt Rebecca Conlon was happy fantasizing about Dale Perry . . .

It seemed that everyone was going along just fine.

Except me.

Quite often, I found myself chanting the word *misery*, like the pitiful creature I was.

I whinged inside.

I whined.

I whimpered.

I scratched at my insides.

Then I laughed.

At myself.

It happened when I was out in the evening, after dinner.

The sausages and mushrooms were settling in my stomach and amongst all the anguish I was carrying around, a very weird laughter broke through me. As I lifted my feet over the ground, I smiled and eventually placed my hand on a telegraph pole to rest.

Standing there, I allowed the laughter to come out of me, and people coming past must have thought I was crazy or drugged or something like that. They looked at me as if to say, 'What are you laughin' at?' They walked on quickly, though, towards their own lives, as I stood paused amongst mine.

That was when I decided that I had to decide something.

I had to decide what I was going to do, and what I was going to be.

I was standing there, waiting for someone to do something, till I realized the person I was waiting for was myself.

Everything inside me was numb, vaguely alive, almost as if it wasn't daring to move, waiting on my decision.

I breathed out and said, 'OK.'

That was all it took.

One word, and sprinting home, I knew that what I was going to do was make it back, clean myself up a bit, and run the five kilometres to Rebecca Conlon's place and ask if she wanted to do something on the weekend. Who cared what anyone thought? I didn't care what Mum or Dad would say, what Rube or Steve would say, what Sarah would say, or what *you* would say. I just knew that this was what I had to do.

'Right now,' I emphasized as I ran, forcing my shoulders forward and going like I was after a fake rabbit. Sickness swept over me as I ran, as if food was turning to acid. Still, though, I ran harder and jumped our front gate and into our house to find.

Sarah on the phone.

Phone.

*Yes, phone*, I thought. *Of course.* Running all the way there and talking to her face-to-face seemed pretty scary by now, so the new plan was to get to a phone box somewhere. I got some change out of my drawer, wrote down the Conlon number on my hand from Dad's work pad, and ran back out for the nearest phone box.

'Oi!' A voice followed me onto the footpath. It

was Steve, from the porch. I hadn't even noticed him when I'd come charging into the house. 'Where y' goin'?'

I stopped, but I didn't answer his question. I walked back to him quickly, suddenly remembering what he'd said to me the last time he'd spoken from the porch, the night Rube and I returned the giveway sign.

'You guys are such losers.' That's what he'd said, and now I walked up our steps and pointed a finger at him as he leaned on the railing and stretched.

I pointed at him and said, 'If you ever call me a loser again, I'm gonna smash your face in.' I meant it, and I could see from the look on his face that he knew I meant it. He even smiled, like he knew something. 'I'm a fighter,' I concluded, 'not a loser. There's a difference.'

My eyes stayed in his for barely another moment. I meant it all right. I meant every word. Steve enjoyed it. I enjoyed it more.

Phone box.

I took off again, obsessed.

The only problem now with the phone box plan was that I couldn't exactly find one. I thought there was one at a particular spot on Elizabeth Street but it had been taken away. I could only keep running, this time in the direction of the Conlon place, until about three kilometres later, I found one. Had I run another two kilometres I could have talked to her in person after all.

'Oh, mate.' I stuck my hands on my knees when I made it to the phone. 'Mate,' and I knew very abruptly that running there had been the easy part. Now I had to dial the number and talk.

My fingers were claws on the ancient dialler as I called up the number, and . . .

Waited.

'. . . ing.'

It was ringing.

'Noth-ing.'

'Noth-ing.'

'Noth-ing.'

She didn't answer and I had to explain to the person who did exactly who I was.

'Cameron.'

'Cameron?'

'Cameron Wolfe, y' silly old cow!' I felt like screaming, but I kept myself back. Instead, I said with quiet dignity, 'Cameron Wolfe. I work with the plumber.' I realized after speaking those words that I was still very much out of breath. I was panting into the telephone, even when Rebecca Conlon was finally on the other end.

'Rebecca?'

'Yeah?'

The voice, her voice.

Hers.

I stuttered things out, but not dumbstruck. I concentrated, and it was all done with purpose, with desire, almost with a severe, serene pride. My voice crawled to her. It asked. Squashing the phone. Go on. Do it. Ask.

'Yeah, I was wonderin' . . .'

My throat hurt.

'Wonderin' if . . .'

Saturday.

That would be the day.

No.

No?

Yes, *no* — you heard me.

Although, Rebecca Conlon didn't say the word *no* when she rejected me for some kind of meeting between us on Saturday. She said, 'I can't,' and I look back now and wonder if the disappointment in her voice was genuine.

Of course I wonder, because she went on to tell me that she couldn't do anything on Sunday or the next weekend either because of some kind of family thing, or another thing of some description. No point pretending. She was giving herself some good safe ground to keep me at bay. See, I hadn't even asked her about Sunday yet. Or the next weekend! The pain in my ear counted at me. The black sky above me seemed to come down. I felt like I was sucking in the grey clouds that stood above, and very slowly, the phone call faded out.

'Well, maybe some other time.' I smiled viciously inside the dirty phone box. My voice was still nice, though, and dignified.

'Yeah, that'd be great, ay.' Nice, great voice. The last time I would hear it? Probably, unless she was dumb enough to be at her house on the upcoming weekend when Dad and I would finish the job.

Yes, her voice, and somehow, I couldn't be sure if it was so real to me any more. It was too far out of reach now to be real.

'Ok, I'll see y' later,' I finished, but I wasn't seeing anyone later.

'OK, bye-ee,' adding insult to injury.

Hearing her hang up then was brutal. I listened

hard and the sound was something ripping apart my head. Slowly, slowly I dropped the receiver down to leave it hanging there, half dead.

Caught.

Tried.

Hanged.

I left it hanging there and walked away, home.

The way back wasn't as bad as you might think, because thoughts fighting in my head made the time go past quickly. Every step left an invisible print on the footpath, which only I could smell on my way past in the future. Good luck.

Halfway there I noticed another phone box in a side street, sitting there joking me and laughing.

'Huh,' was all I said to myself, as I kept walking and eased an itch on my shoulder blade with a tired hand stretching at the end of a bent, twisting elbow

This time, I staggered into the front gate, stayed around a while, and went to bed at about ten-thirty.

I didn't sleep.

I sweated, shivering, alone.

I saw things, plastered down onto my eyes.

Thrown into them.

I saw it all. Every detail. From a baseball and cricket bat, fluoride treatment, an empty signpost, dreams, fathers, brothers, mother, sister, Bruce, friend, girl, voice, gone, and into. Me.

My life trampled my bed.

I felt tears like hammers down my face.

I saw myself walking to that phone. Talking. Staggering home.

Then, close to one o'clock, I stood up and put my jeans on and walked barefoot out into the back yard.

Out of our room.

Down the hallway.

Out the back door.

Freezing cold night.

Past the cement and onto the grass, till I stood.

I stood there and stared, into the sky and at the city around me. I stood, hands at my side, and I saw what had happened to me and who I was and the way things would always be for me. Truth. There was no more wishing, or wondering. I knew who I was, and what I would always do. I believed it, as my teeth touched and my eyes were overrun.

My mouth opened. It happened.

Yes, with my head thrown into the sky, I started howling.

Arms stretched out next to me, I howled, and

everything came out of me. Visions poured up my throat and past voices surrounded me. The sky listened. The city didn't. I didn't care. All I cared about was that I was howling so that I could hear my voice and so I would remember that the boy had intensity and something to offer. I howled, oh, so loud and desperate, telling a world that I was here and I wouldn't lie down.

Not tonight.

Not ever.

Yes, I howled and without me knowing it, my family stood just beyond the back door, watching me and wondering what I was doing.

*At first, all is black and white. Black on white.*

*That's where I'm walking, through pages.*

*These pages.*

*Sometimes it gets so that I have one foot in the pages and the words, and the other in what they speak of.*

*Sometimes I'm there again, hatching plans with Rube, fighting him, working with Dad, getting called a wild animal by my mother, watching Sarah's life stumble at the hands of Bruce, and telling Steve I'll smash his face in if he ever calls me a loser again. I even see Greg's bought* stash going up through his chimney, drugging the air above his roof. One foot walks me towards Rebecca Conlon's place and working there, and ringing there. One foot stands me in the picture where the strangled public telephone hangs, dead, with only the remains of my voice left inside it.

Sometimes, when I am deep inside the pages, the letters of every word are like the huge buildings of the city. I stand beneath them, looking up.

I run at times.

I crawl.

Through.

Every page.

Dreams cover me sometimes, but at others, they strip the flesh off my soul or take the blanket away from me, leaving me with just myself, cold.

Fingers touch the pages.

They turn me.

I continue on.

I always do.

All is big.

The pages and the words are my world, spread out before your eyes and for your hands to touch. Vaguely, I can see your face looking down into me, as I look back. Do you see my eyes?

Still, I walk on, through a dream that takes me through these pages.

I arrive at the point where I see myself walking out to the back yard into the freezing cold. I see city and sky, and I feel the cold. I stand next to myself.

Jeans.

Bare feet.

Bare chest, shivering.

Boys' arms.

They're stretched out, reaching.

A wind picks up and sheets of paper take flight and fall down around us as we stand there. A howling noise stumbles despairingly for my ears and I receive it.

I hang on to that desperation, because.

I need it.

I want it.

I smile.

Dogs bark, far away but coming closer.

Next to me, I hear myself howl.

This is a good dream.

Howling. Loud.

Intense.

The last sheets of paper still fall.

I'm alive.

*I've never been so—*

*I look down.*

*The words are my life.*

*Howling continues.*

*I stand with pages strewn at my ankles and with that howling in my ears.*

## ABOUT THE AUTHOR

Markus Zusak is the author of five novels,
including the internationally bestselling
*The Book Thief*, which is translated into
over thirty languages.

He lives in Sydney with his wife and daughter.

Also available by

# MARKUS ZUSAK

and published by Definitions

The Wolfe brothers know how to fight. They've been fighting all their lives. Now there's something more at stake than just winning.

'An impressive and heartwarming story
of fraternal and familial bonding'
*Irish Times*

Cameron and Ruben have always been loyal brothers.
That is until Cam falls for Octavia
– Rube's latest girlfriend.

But she would never go for a guy like Cameron anyway.
Would she?

This is the tale of the book thief, as narrated by death.
And when death tells a story, you really have to listen.

'Extraordinary, resonant and relevant,
beautiful and angry'
*Telegraph*